Praise for
THE MEANS

"A fast-paced and funny send-up."

"Delicious."

—Zibby Owe.   ...gAmerica.com

"A plucky jaunt of a novel."

—*The New York Times Book Review*

"With its deadpan absurdity, pithy prose, and moral je ne sais quoi, Fusselman's latest will appeal to fans of Marcy Dermansky. . . . With its satire of the particular hypocrisy of the Hamptons, including homeowners associations, graft, and garbage and recycling practices, Maria Semple. . . . We may be entering a golden age of the comic novel, surely one of the best possible outcomes of this desperate moment in history."

—*Kirkus Reviews* (starred review)

"Just like its title, Amy Fusselman's new novel is breezy sharp, super funny, and full of second meanings and surprising insights into "The Means," and what it means to have and lack them. You don't have to want to live in a shipping container in the Hamptons to understand Shelly Means and the yearnings that drive her hilarious desperate measures. But if you need a hint, Twix the socialist dog will yell it at you. (SPOILER but look: Maria Semple and David Sedaris are brilliant, but have they written a talking dog as funny as Twix? The answer, my friends, is no. You can only find this, and so much else, in *The Means*)."

—John Hodgman, author of *Vacationland: True Stories from Painful Beaches* and *Medallion Status: True Stories from Secret Rooms*

"This charming novel bears the Fusselman touch that makes all of her books so brilliant: touching, uncanny, and deceptively simple observations that dismantle complex assumptions about the world."

—Sarah Manguso, author of *Very Cold People*

"Amy Fusselman's *The Means* is an absolute delight! Anyone who's ever wanted more than they had—so, all of us—will be unable to turn away from this wise, funny, page-turning story of relationships, motherhood, and real estate ambitions."

—Jessica Anya Blau, author of *Mary Jane*

"'Location, location, location': That is the real estate chant. In Amy Fusselman's *The Means,* those words are intermingled with 'laugh, laugh, laugh.' Fusselman is a prescient observer, chronicling one couple's desire to live near where the other half lives. She deftly captures the absurdity of the everyday and the American quest for more. *The Means* is funny, playful, and at times painfully accurate."

—A. M. Homes, author of *The Unfolding* and *May We Be Forgiven*

"*The Means* is such a fast-paced, breezy comedic novel that you may find yourself surprised that Fusselman deftly and directly leads you to existential dilemmas and the absurdity of capitalism and striving for more."

—The Millions

"Fusselman (*Idiophone,* 2018) delivers a well-paced story with gentle humor, compassion, and a sparkling, original look at the absurdities of everyday life in a world filled with inequities, financial and otherwise."

—*Booklist*

"[An] entertaining debut. . . . Recommended to anyone who enjoys humorous fiction."

—*Library Journal*

"Damn funny. . . . Fusselman presents a hilariously heightened reality."

—Shelf Awareness

The Means

The Means

Amy Fusselman

MARINER BOOKS

New York   Boston

HarperCollins books may be purchased for educational, business, or sales promotional use. For information, please email the Special Markets Department at SPsales@harpercollins.com.

A hardcover edition of this book was published in 2022 by Mariner Books.

FIRST MARINER BOOKS PAPERBACK EDITION PUBLISHED 2023.

Designed by Emily Snyder

Library of Congress Cataloging-in-Publication Data

Names: Fusselman, Amy, author.
Title: The means / Amy Fusselman.
Description: Boston : Mariner Books, [2022]
Identifiers: LCCN 2022017391 (print) | LCCN 2022017392 (ebook) | ISBN 9780063248717 (hardcover) | ISBN 9780063248724 (paperback) | ISBN 9780063248731 (ebook)
Subjects: LCGFT: Novels.
Classification: LCC PS3606.U86 M43 2022 (print) | LCC PS3606.U86 (ebook) | DDC 813/.6—dc23
LC record available at https://lccn.loc.gov/2022017391
LC ebook record available at https://lccn.loc.gov/2022017392

ISBN 978-0-06-324872-4

23 24 25 26 27 LBC 5 4 3 2 1

For Katie, Lyons, and King

The Means

Pre-Winter

~~~~

1

MUST-HAVES:
Japanese toilet
4 beds
3 baths
Heated pool
Heated floors
Garage

At last! I am going to get a beach house!

STEPS I HAVE TAKEN TO GET TO THIS
MOMENT OF BEACH HOUSE OWNERSHIP:
+ Born
+ Childhood
+ College
+ Married (George)

✦ George made $$$

✦ George and I bought lake house

✦ A raccoon wedged its beefy body through a hole that we didn't know existed in the lake house chimney guard. He fell down the chimney into the house when we weren't there and then spent a week drinking out of the toilet, jumping on the beds, and smearing soot on every surface. He was like a coin that dropped into the slot machine of our lake house, causing a riot of spinning fruits and ringing bells.

We had no idea we were winning like this. We had no camera installed. Our observant neighbor at the lake called us at our apartment in the city to tell us about our jackpot. He advised us to call the wildlife control people, so I did that. And then the wildlife control people went out to the house and after three long days they called me back and said, "The bad news is that you have a raccoon in your house, and the other bad news is we can't get him out."

"Look at that," I said to George, who was sitting beside me in the kitchen in our apartment on West Twenty-Seventh Street, in what we fondly referred to as the discount caftan and incense district. "The wildlife control people can't control the wildlife, just like us."

I then called different wildlife control people I had searched up—who knew there were so many of them in that little lake town, like they were pizza joints—and these other wildlife control people must have been PhD-level animal behaviorists because they opened our front door and put bait outside it, and just like that, our raccoon—because we thought of him as ours now—walked out the front door and back into his life again. And then I hope he drank many raccoon beers with his raccoon friends and told them all about the time he fell down a hole into another world and went berserk there until a door opened and he walked out of it, a changed animal.

George and I were English majors in college, and we had met in a class on Charles Dickens, so we thought we were prepared—in a fictional, chimney-sweep-loving way—for cleaning up after a sooty raccoon. But our nonfiction raccoon had not only fallen down our lake house chimney, he had cut himself on a glass jar of organic peanut butter that he had smashed open, so in addition to chimney soot and peanut butter, raccoon blood was everywhere, and it was that last little detail that pushed the entire situation out of the realm of Victorian literature and into the territory of a horror film. Cleaning bloody paw prints from the ceiling was not at all like writing a five-paragraph essay about Oliver Twist and his dual role as a victim and thief.

After George and I cleaned, then hired a service to clean up extra after our cleaning, we came to the conclusion that it was time to sell the lake house. We hardly went there anymore because we were so busy; we couldn't deal with the homeowner issues; and the younger of our two kids, our ten-year-old daughter, Clementine, having learned to swim in the YMCA pool, refused to swim in the lake whenever she saw "gunk" in it, which was always, because although Clementine can't remember her times tables very well, she has the visual acuity of a bird of prey.

We sold our raccoon-haunted house, and then we did something only real winners could do, which was spend all our lake house money on a small plot of land in East Hampton. The plot of land was in what is arguably the most down-market part of East Hampton, the area that contains the dump *and* has the spottiest cell phone service. It's known as "Springs," or "The Springs," depending on how you say it. People who have lived in the area for a long time tend to say "Springs," whereas people who are new say "The Springs," and the people who say "Springs" reportedly think that the people who say "The Springs" are insufferable. I will be referring to it as "The Springs," though, because I am not trying to be anyone I am not here.

For a long time, then, we had this bit of land in The Springs with no dwelling on it, just a slightly dented black metal mailbox on a wooden post that George had gotten from a nearby garage sale. He plunked it at the edge of the land, on the spot where we dreamed of putting the driveway that would lead to our house. On the side of the mailbox he painted yellow and orange flames like the ones on the demolition derby cars he had loved as a kid, and then he painted our name in red-hot letters: MEANS.

Eventually, after searching, I found an architect who said she could make us a house on this land for cheap. The price she quoted us was so cheap, in fact, that it seemed unreal, like the price equivalent of a raccoon drinking beer with his raccoon friends. But maybe this is my problem, being a former English major: I like a good story. So I listened to this architect give me her pitch, and I thought, well, this could happen.

2

I WAS SITTING ON the couch in my sweatpants looking for pictures of heated swimming pools to put on my vision board when Darby let herself into our third-floor apartment to walk the dog.

"Hi, Darby," I said, slightly tilting my laptop screen so she couldn't see it.

"Looking at swimming pools again, Shelly?" she asked, as she picked up our twelve-pound, caramel-colored dog, Twix.

Darby was skinny, sarcastic, and all of twenty-three. She was wearing her cool-weather ensemble of a hoodie-over-a-hoodie. She hated coats and swore that hoodies were enough to get her through New York City's five seasons: pre-winter, winter, second winter, slush, and summer.

"Your observational skills are scary," I replied, as Twix looked at me balefully from the crook of her arm.

"Well, I'm not *trying* to be scary," she replied, glancing at me over her shoulder as she put the leash on the dog. "But if you *are* scared, that's fine."

I asked myself, was I scared of Darby, a Fashion Institute of Technology student who walked dogs on the side? I answered myself: No.

In addition to pools, I had tabs open for refrigerators that spit ice cubes out the door, fireplaces that turned on with the push of a button, and toilets that flushed themselves and then sprayed your bottom clean. I was delirious with excitement about my new beach house and all its new accoutrements.

"You don't have to feel guilty about getting a beach house, you know," Darby said.

"I don't feel guilty about getting a beach house," I snapped. "Besides, it's going to be the cheapest beach house imaginable. It's going to be made out of shipping containers. It's going to look like a big metal box!"

"That's how I know you feel guilty," she said, smirking. "Otherwise you'd be telling me how nice it is." She walked out the door with Twix.

I stopped my pool perusal and remembered how, when I was nine and my older sister, Bella, was fifteen, my family went on a vacation. My father drove us nine hours from our home in Minneapolis to the Black Hills. I had been alarmed by this trip, which was done with so much resentment, and was so joyless, and took so long. It seemed pointless, although I knew the point, which was to "get away" and "take a break" and "relax" from our regular lives as an unremarkable, white, Midwestern family where everyone worked hard, money didn't come easily, and you couldn't buy things from the dollar store because that was something only poor people did. We were not poor people, we were practical people, my father reminded us, cracking open his sixth beer in half as many hours behind the steering wheel of our compact car.

We'd stayed in a cheap motel overnight. As soon as we checked in, it started pouring, and then continued raining all the next day. My sister and I were bored and whining. My father decided we would leave our vacation early. The gutters on our house would be backed up after all this rain, and he would need to clean them, he groused.

My father drove us back home in the storm, grim and hungover, and then we never took another family vacation, let alone another vacation to the Black Hills, which was fine. Especially because vacationing to the Black Hills, as I now know, is a morally complicated activity.

I looked up from the computer to see Darby and Twix come back inside. Darby wiped the sidewalk crud off Twix's feet with a baby wipe from the box of wipes by the door. Then she nodded at me and left.

I employ Darby through a company called Canine Companions. They require their employees to take photos of the dogs as they are walking them. These photos are then included in an email that gets sent when the walk is over. The email tells me exactly how long the walk was and if my dog did #1, #2, or both.

The post-dog-walk email came. In her 30:07-minute walk up and down West Twenty-Seventh Street, Twix had made zero numbers.

3

DARBY WALKS TWIX Monday through Friday mornings so I can get some work done. I have a job that, as far as the wider working world is concerned, is not real: taking care of two children. The wider working world's opinion of my job used to bother me, but it doesn't anymore. I don't care what the world thinks, I tell myself.

Darby walks Twix in the morning, and then I walk Twix the other two times a day, or sometimes George, or our son, Jack, who's sixteen, walks her. Clementine, at ten, is too young to walk the dog alone on our block, which is on Twenty-Seventh between Sixth and Seventh Avenues. We're right down the block from the Fashion Institute of Technology, where Darby, who dreams of having her own accessories line one day, is taking a class called "Manipulating Leather 2."

George and I found our two-bedroom apartment on this block for a good price. We bought it when I was pregnant with Jack. And then after Clementine was born, when other people might have prioritized moving to a bigger apartment, we decided to spend our money on a raccoon Airbnb.

Still, we have managed to make our apartment work for four people. Both kids are in one bedroom, which we turned into two bedrooms with the help of an illegal wall that will have to come down if we ever try to sell the apartment. We constructed it without running it past our co-op board.

Our apartment is in Chelsea, but our stretch of West Twenty-Seventh Street is not the Chelsea of charming, pedigreed town houses. Our block is filled with ground- and second-floor businesses. If you want to learn martial arts, take an improv comedy class, or buy a ten-dollar caftan, come to my block. Our building is next to a store called IBS Enterprise, which sells everything from luggage to snow globes, and which George and I refer to as "Irritable Bowel Syndrome."

If Irritable Bowel Syndrome wasn't enough Manhattan shopping fabulousness for one neighborhood, there is also what you might generously call a "pop-up" on the Sixth Avenue end of our block. It's basically a weekly rummage sale anchored by a couple of legitimate antique sellers, as well as a crabby guy in a dashiki who sells incense with names like "Sensual Nights" and "Dragon's Blood." I bought Dragon's Blood once because Clementine begged me—and who doesn't want to know what dragon's blood smells like?—so we found out: burned cinnamon toast. We have learned to hold our breath as we walk through the clouds emanating from the incense guy's table, because if he hears you making any negative comments, he will yell at you using, as Clementine calls them, "potty words."

Twix takes her walks in this landscape. She is not a big fan of her walks, but she goes on them dutifully, like they're her job, like they're a vacation to the Black Hills she is being taken on because she is a small child in a family that does not understand vacations, and she has no choice.

While she is out for her morning walk, I usually eat because it is easier to eat treats when you don't have a dog around. Twix's walks with Darby are a half-hour long. That gives me more than enough time to eat some chocolate, which I eat from a bag of chocolate chips I keep in the pantry. I dig out the chips in handfuls and eat them like a squirrel.

4

I SOMETIMES MAKE THE mistake of adding more jobs to my not-real workload. Several years ago, for instance, the head of my kids' private school asked me if I would volunteer to be the PTA president and I said OK even though I didn't want to. But I said yes because we were a financial-aid family and I didn't want to screw that up.

I would never have considered applying for financial aid—did we not have an apartment in the caftan and incense district as well as a raccoon Airbnb?—but one of George's work buddies, Ted, advised him to. Ted was an older guy who had put his two grown children through multiple New York City private schools, and he raised his eyebrows when George told him we were applying for privates for Jack for sixth grade. He said as long as we were applying, we might want to try for aid, because "you never know."

Ted was implying that George's job was precarious, which was true, although we never thought of it that way. Ted also advised George that we should apply to as many places as possible because

New York City private school admissions were insanely competitive and we were at a disadvantage because we "didn't know anyone."

I took offense to that last statement, but George explained that Ted meant only that we didn't know anyone already in a private school who could help Jack get in. We did know about doing financial-aid paperwork, though, because both George and I had gone to college with financial aid. So in another one of my jobs, I filled out all the forms and submitted them.

Ted had forgotten to mention the importance of a serious investment in test prep, so we didn't do that for Jack, and he didn't do a great job on the private school entrance exam. All the privates he applied to rejected him except one, the Chase School, which had recently had a major sex scandal involving a senior class trip to Tulum. Chase not only accepted Jack, they gave us a break on tuition, so that's where he went, and that's where I got my PTA gig.

I had a major mishap on that job, though. During a board meeting, I got so frustrated with Kevin, the finance bro who was the head of the school's board of trustees, that I threw my new, self-cleaning water bottle at him. It didn't hit him; it hit the wall behind him. But that was the end of my PTA career.

After The Incident, as George and I referred to it afterward, George gave me two choices: individual therapy or anger-management classes. I chose therapy because it seemed easier. Anger-management classes sounded like there might be homework.

It was my job to find my therapist, so I searched around online and found someone who did cognitive behavioral therapy, which appealed to me, because it seemed like it might be more like exercise and less like crying. The goal of C.B.T., as I understood it, was to train your thoughts, like your thoughts were a puppy who was chewing your shoes. It was obedience classes for your thoughts, basically. After successfully completing the training, you would think things like, "I am experiencing a cognitive distortion right now," instead of "I want to punch Kevin in the face."

I found a therapist named Alice. She checked all the boxes for me. She had graduated from an authorized C.B.T. certification program, her rates were pretty low, and she did sessions on her device. George said he would have preferred that I work with a "real" doctor, in a "real" office, but real doctors in real offices are expensive, I reminded him, and the health insurance he got from work didn't cover that kind of therapy.

Alice is easy to talk to, anyway. At therapy today, on my screen, I told her how I like buying new things, and she asked me why, and I said because new things seem real, and she asked me when do new things seem the most real to you, and I said when I see them in advertisements.

One of my favorite things to look at, in an advertisement, is a little round jar of face cream. I like the ones with shiny, silver lids on top and exotic ingredients, like propolis extract, inside. I looked it up: propolis extract comes from bees.

An unopened jar of face cream arrives in a sealed box, so perfect, so silver. It's like a little spaceship you fly by, opening it up, dipping your fingers into it, and then smearing your cream-covered fingers on your face.

I like to put on face cream in the morning before tackling my many jobs. Besides taking care of everyone, I also buy everything we need, do all our paperwork, and organize all our activities. Plus, I also have another job now, which is doing everything to make this beach house appear except making the money to pay for it.

I complained to Alice about that in therapy. I told her that I was working so hard on this beach house project that I was worried that I was not exuding enough joy about it and that maybe my sorrowful past working as a child in the blacking factory—wait, no, that was Charles Dickens. Maybe my sorrowful past taking one subpar vacation to the Black Hills of South Dakota had ruined me for life.

Alice listened as she fingered her statement jewelry. She is a good-looking white woman in her forties and always wears some sort of sleek, all-black ensemble that she accessorizes with a rock hanging around her neck. Today's pendant was a tangerine-size geode. She fiddled with its pointy parts as she encouraged me to show more enthusiasm for the beach house. For one thing, she suggested, I could stop calling it "The Tin Can" in casual conversation, because that was mocking it. It pained me to let go of this name, though, because "The Tin Can" was perfect, not only because the house was going to be made of metal, but because it was going to be weird, and "Here . . . am I floating 'round my tin can," is a line from David Bowie's masterpiece "Space Oddity," and that's about as perfect a weird metal space reference as you can get.

As a step toward displaying more openheartedness toward my house, though, I decided, with Alice's help, that I would send an email to Bea, the president of the Silver Sound Homeowner's Association. Silver Sound was the little enclave near the beach in The Springs where our land was located. I couldn't take that name seriously, so I had been calling it Crashing Sound whenever I talked about it.

George and I got emails from Bea all the time. She was a white retiree who lived a couple of streets over from where our land was. She wrote to all the owners in the association—about eighty people total—alerting them to lost dogs, reminding them to remove their kayaks from the beach when summer was over, and inviting them to housing association cocktail parties, which seemed to be held every other weekend. We never went to those parties because we didn't live there. We had no home to live in (yet).

I thought I could send an email to Bea and tell her that we had chosen an architect and that construction on our house would begin soon. And then maybe Bea would respond with "Congratulations!" and we would have a little bonding moment.

I wrote:

Dear Bea, I am happy to share the news that we have finally chosen an architect and will soon be breaking ground on our house. Our home will be made of shipping containers and will be really beautiful. You can see pictures of other homes like this here.

I included a link. Then I sent it and sat back, feeling expansive, like I was making some progress.

It did not take five minutes before my device dinged.

Dear Mr. and Mrs. Means, That type of home does not belong in Silver Sound. Are you planning on coming to our next cocktail party? We are trying to raise money to hire an attendant for our clubhouse.

I called George at work, hysterical.

"Calm down," George said. "She's just trolling you."

Still, I did what people who can afford tin can beach houses do in these situations, which is leave a message for our real estate lawyer. And then, as I was waiting for the call back, I posted a picture of my favorite Japanese toilet on social media.

5

THE NEXT MORNING, George was headed to the studio to record a commercial. He is a voice-over artist and had been cast as the voice of a new chicken sandwich. The ad was going to run all over the country. Ka-ching! We were psyched.

George has a lot of money now, which is not how he grew up, as a kid in Dorchester. I think George always knew he was going to make money, though. He knew it was possible. He wasn't like me, someone who grew up with some money but never felt like it and thus was conflicted about it.

George is not conflicted about money. When money comes his way, he doesn't view it warily or shut it out or apologize for it or feel guilty about it. He just says yes, thank you.

For example, when George moved to New York City after college, he ran into a friend on Lexington Avenue who asked if he would take a temporary job as a receptionist at his office, because the receptionist was going on vacation and George has a very nice voice.

That was an important first "yes" that George said. Because that office was a swanky film-editing company with expensive bottled drinks in the fridge, a candy drawer for clients, and a catered lunch every day. All George had to do was sit there and say "Hello?" into the headset, and when he wasn't doing that, he could just say "More, please" at lunch, and he would get more, no problem. It was the most un-Dickensian introduction to the working world imaginable.

And then one day the guys who were editing film needed someone to come in and do a quick voice-over on spec, and they asked George if he could jump in, and he said yes again. And the clients loved George's placeholder voice and asked him to join the Screen Actors Guild so he could record the lines for real, for money, and he said yes to that, too. And then after a few years of doing occasional jobs here and there while I worked at the bookstore, Jack was born, and then, a few years after that, George ended up being the voice in that burger commercial that was broadcast in every format, in every corner of the country, for over a year.

And that is how George went from being a part-time receptionist to being a full-time voice-over guy, or as full-time as that gets, because voice-over work is one of the highest minute-per-dollar types of work you can get, next to, like, being a neurosurgeon.

I sat on our bed, watching him get ready. He was doing vocal warm-up exercises where he breathed in deeply and then exhaled while saying "HA HA HA" like a laughing robot.

"Good luck," I said.

"HA HA HA," he replied, putting on his lucky voice-over socks, the ones I had ordered with pictures of Twix's face printed on them because if you go into the way back of Irritable Bowel Syndrome, you will discover that they have a full-service custom printing operation.

I checked the likes on my Japanese toilet post as he finished getting dressed. "I have so many comments on my toilet!" I exclaimed.

"What kind of comments?"

I read aloud:

U R TOO DUMB TO USE THIS TOILET
UR TOILET IS ASS
WHY ARE U ALIVE

"Whoa! I have trolls!" I exclaimed.

"I guess that happens," George said dryly.

I told myself again that this was why I shouldn't be on social media. It seemed like it was taking me several tries to learn this. I had already sworn off posting pictures of my kids. I had discovered that this was an unusual approach to have as a mother, though. It was as if the only legitimate way to experience parental pride was by running images of your kids through the heart-and-like economy.

George is not on social media. He is on his device all the time, but he isn't liking things. He's usually researching prices of things.

"Where did the trolls come from?" I was miffed.

"I've heard that toilet photos attract them," George replied. "They're like catnip, but for trolls."

Sometimes George makes fun of my habit of asking him questions like he is a search engine by spewing nonsense at me in the same tone that he uses to tell me correct information. Usually we laugh at this together, but at this particular moment, it wasn't funny.

"Are trolls even alive?" I fumed. "Aren't some of them just robots?"

George sometimes ignores my search engine questions if he thinks they're too ridiculous. He did that ignoring now. I turned away from him sulkily. I was not very happy about this takedown of my toilet. This toilet was a dream of mine. I had become obsessed with these toilets after going to Tokyo with George before we had kids. I could not believe that such appliances existed. You could poop and pee on a toilet that would play cheerful music to cover up your activities, clean and dry your butt, and then flush your master-piece away when it sensed you standing up. It was like being a dog and having your own dog walker tend to all your numbers.

In Tokyo, these toilets weren't exclusively available at high-end hotels, and I knew that because we didn't stay at any high-end hotels. These toilets were in the stalls of the giant arena where we went to watch sumo wrestling. The equivalent would be if these toilets were installed in every single toilet stall at Madison Square Garden. That's how amazing Tokyo is.

When I came home from that trip, it took me a while to get used to the fact that I had to flush the toilet myself. I wanted someone else to deal with it: a music-playing, ass-cleaning robot. I vowed I would one day get a Japanese toilet for myself.

I had envisioned my Japanese toilet being installed in our beach house bathroom because I didn't want to share it with our kids. I had chosen one already off the Toto site. Of course the maker of this toilet is named after another great dog, I thought. This partic-ular model appealed to me because it had a remote. I was already scheming about how I was going to take the remote, and then when George went into the bathroom, I was going to use the remote from outside the bathroom to turn on the butt spray when he was least expecting it.

6

WHEN DARBY CAME in a little later, I was still moodily contemplating my post.

"Hi, Darby," I said, looking up.

"Hi, Shelly," she replied, munching a Caring bar. I've had those before. They're gross.

I watched as she scooped up Twix and left. It was sometimes hard for me to believe that I had broken down and gotten a dog. My kids had begged for a dog for years, but I was one of those moms who did not want a dog for all the usual reasons moms do not want dogs. Plus, I had had a childhood dog, and I knew that if I ever got a dog in adulthood, my childhood dog would come back and haunt me immediately. I was happy just as I was, with no real dog and no ghost dog.

My childhood dog was a dachshund named Julie. My mother picked her out, and my mother named her. My mother hated her in-laws, and she named the dog Julie after my cousin. My mother would never admit to this, though. When my uncle complained about my mother naming our dog the same name as his daughter, my mother said it was just a coincidence. This particular miniature dachshund just looked like a Julie, that was all.

I only saw the human Julie a couple of times a year. I lived with the dog Julie for many years, but my memory of her is fuzzy. What I remember most about her is that my mother kept her cookies on the counter, in full view of the world, naked and unashamed. My father sometimes popped one of these cookies into his mouth after dinner, to my mother's horror.

I finally had my come-to-Jesus dog moment, though, with an animal who was not a dog, named Tim. Tim was a sea lion I met in Atlantis, where I had insisted my family go on vacation after George had accrued enough miles on his credit card to get us there for free.

I met Tim at a "sea lion interaction" I bought for Jack while George and Clementine went down the lazy river. I didn't buy a sea lion interaction for myself. I was doing that parent-in-Atlantis thing where you get all the way to a mythical paradise and then complain about the price of swimming with dolphins.

The sea lion handler let me sit on a bench and watch, so I was there when Tim waddled out from his private tank, and I was there to watch him jump through hoops, give high fives, and dance the conga with his trainer, which was actually pretty unnerving, because it seemed like they had trained all the animal out of him, which I guess was the point.

I remember thinking that if Tim were a raccoon who had fallen down our lake house chimney, he probably would not have spent a week drinking out of the toilet and bleeding on the bathroom ceiling. He would have sat there calmly, like a well-behaved kindergartner, until someone came by and dropped off his monogrammed, fish-filled lunch box.

When Tim was done performing for us, his trainer said we could pet him, and by this he meant I could pet him, too. I wanted to pet

Tim, but I was afraid to pet Tim. Tim was 450 pounds. His teeth were huge. He ate twenty-four pounds of fish a day, the trainer had told us.

"Just touch his back and not his head and he won't attack you," the trainer said, which did not make me feel calmer.

Jack had no such issues; he petted Tim.

Tim showed all his teeth as Jack touched him. Maybe he was smiling? I watched him warily.

It was my turn; I put my hand very gently on Tim's gargantuan back. As soon as I touched him, I started to cry. It was a crying that did not come with any thoughts or words attached to it. It just suddenly and with no forewarning fell down my chimney and walked out of my eyes. And then it was like every animal on earth—including Julie, who was long dead—came to me in a flood, like I was experiencing Noah's ark backward, as a joyful release of all the animals, rather than a gathering-up and shutting-in of them.

After I came home from Atlantis, I could no longer say no to any puppies my kids admired at the puppy store. So the next time I took the kids to the puppy store, they picked out a dog and we brought her home. She was 25 percent off, which cinched it. And sometimes when George is petting her, he will tell her in a baby voice that she was on sale and that's why we bought her. And then I will scold him for being mean to the dog, and he will argue that she doesn't understand him, and I will say yes, she does, and the dog will look at us in a way that I say is fully comprehending and George will say is meaningless, and we go on in this manner until one of us gets tired, because the only one who could stop us from disagreeing about this is Twix, and she says nothing on the topic.

And if there weren't already enough things that I feel guilty about, I also feel guilty that we got our dog from a puppy store, because, as my dear friends have so kindly clued me in, we bought our dog all wrong. If I were going to buy a dog in the right way, I would have gotten a rescue dog. I could even have sprung for a double, or even a triple rescue, I know now, because dogs, like humans, can have horrible life experiences multiple times and may need to be rescued exponentially.

But it's too late for me to give my dog back for a dog with a better, by which I mean worse, backstory. But when people ask me if our dog is a rescue now, I know enough to say yes, yes, she is. We rescued her from the window at the puppy store.

Twix is a Teddy Bear breed, which is a mix of Shih Tzu and Bichon. My guess is the breeders called it a Teddy Bear because they couldn't very well sell her as a Shits On. I always thought that if I ever got a dog after Julie, it would look like Snowy from *Tintin*. It would be a heroic-acting dog with its ears always pointing up because it was always listening for crime.

The dog my kids chose, however, is like a light-brownish cloud that changes size and shape depending on how the wind is blowing when you look at her. Plus, her ears are not pointy at all. They are little folded-over flaps that are always askew, so one is always flopped up over the top of her head and you can seemingly see straight into her brain, which I find disturbing.

Worse, she doesn't give a shits-on about crime. She spends her day lying on our sheepskin rug, and she treats it like a giant piece of sheep jerky, which I guess it is. She lies around on that thing all day and munches it with her ears awry and her brain holes distressingly exposed, like her entire head is a manila envelope that won't seal, that warns you, visually: *Don't put anything important in me.*

My kids named her Twix after the candy, which was also disappointing, because I wanted to give her an authoritative name, like Surgeon General. George wanted to name her Mother Teresa because he has what I call a Mother Teresa fixation. George went to Bible summer camp when he was a kid and was also forced to go to church on Sundays, and even though we don't do that now, as a family, he still thinks Mother Teresa is cool. And yes, he knows all that stuff that came out about her being a vulture who used the poor for her own ends, and yes, he also read Christopher Hitchens's critique on her. But he is still a fan. I know better than to argue at this point. I just thank god that when we had our family fight about what to name our dog, our kids won.

7

ONE THING GEORGE loves to do, which doesn't seem like the activity of a person with money, is to pick up junk off the street. He started this in college, but everyone did that in college. You found a coffee table on the sidewalk and carried it home and it went nicely with your decor because your bed was a mattress on the floor and your bookshelves were milk crates.

People grow out of that, but less so in New York City, where trash ebbs and flows but never completely disappears from the sidewalk, and there is always the possibility that someone has put a worthwhile or interesting item on the curb rather than take the time to resell or donate it.

To be fair, George does have a very good eye for junk. He once brought home an ashtray from the Salvation Army because he thought it looked like "something," and then he found out after researching it that it was a super-rare sculpture, possibly by Isamu Noguchi, and there was another one just like it selling on eBay for sixty thousand—60,000!—dollars.

You would think that, having discovered his not-an-ashtray's market value, George would just unload it immediately. But no, George still has it, and he likes to keep me apprised, every few months or so, of its current dollar value, like it's an investment we made after doing diligent research and not just a completely random, value-packed meteor that fell on us from the sky.

All of this is to say that George is a type of hoarder, yes, but a very specific kind. He can spot when something discarded has value, or the possibility of value, and when that happens, he likes to hold on to it, and keep it close, and cuddle it like a puppy that he has rescued from a horrible life.

When he came home from the chicken sandwich gig, he wasn't thinking about junk. I could tell when he walked in the door that something was wrong.

"I've never had a gig go so badly," he said with a groan, throwing his bag down beside the couch. "I don't even think they're going to use me! I think they're going to trash my recording and get someone else!"

"What makes you think so?" I asked.

"It's just the way they dealt with me. I had to say the line a thousand times and I still don't think I gave them what they wanted!"

"I'm sure it wasn't that bad," I said, petting Twix.

"No, you don't know," he said, flopping on the couch beside me. "I choked. I just could not get the line right."

"What was the line?"

"'The new Chicken Bacon Detonator.'" He said it in his voice-over voice.

"Wow," I said. "That's a mouthful."

"I know! And they wanted something from me—and I still don't know what it was! I was sitting in the booth, and Debbie, the copywriter, was trying to direct me, and she goes, 'OK, George, just give it a wry twist.'"

"A wry twist?"

"Exactly! What the hell is that? So I go, 'The new Chicken Bacon Detonator.'" He paused. "Did you hear that?"

"Hear what?"

"The wry twist!"

"Um, no?"

"No, of course you didn't! Because I couldn't get it! I said it the exact same way as I did without the wry twist, and then it just went on like that for two more hours!"

I made a sympathetic sound.

"And then Debbie goes, 'OK, George, just give it a little smile.' So I go, 'The new Chicken Bacon Detonator.'" He looked at me, wild-eyed.

"I didn't really hear the smile," I admitted.

"Of course you didn't! Because I couldn't do that, either! So Debbie is really desperate now, right? So she goes, 'OK, George, how about you just run with it. Just run with it!'" He threw up his hands.

"How do you run with the new Chicken Bacon Detonator?"

"I know! I said, 'The new Chicken Bacon Detonator.'"

"Exactly the same," I confirmed.

"Yes! I must have said 'The new Chicken Bacon Detonator' ten million times!"

"You're being too hard on yourself. I'm sure you said it fine," I said, trying to be consoling.

"No, I really think they're going to try to recast it! I failed at saying the name of a chicken sandwich! What the hell is wrong with me?!" He palmed his forehead.

"Nothing's wrong with you, George." I patted his arm as he slumped beside me. "Maybe you're just not what they were looking for. And you know what else?"

"Don't say it," he said.

I said it anyway: "Mistakes are how we learn."

He moaned. It was a line we always said to the kids.

"You don't understand," he said, putting his head in his hands. "Now I'll be on the sandwich blacklist. And if I'm blacklisted from sandwiches, I'll never get to cars, and cars are the holy grail!"

I didn't realize there was a hierarchy built into the types of products you could give voice to, but the longer I am alive, the more I realize there is a hierarchy to everything.

George got up from the couch, rubbing the back of his neck, and walked to the kitchen for a drink. I saw that Twix was chewing George's balled-up socks with her face on them.

"No, girl," I scolded her, and took them away.

8

WHEN I GOT Alice on my device for my next therapy appointment, I told her about Bea nixing our shipping container beach house. I told her this because aside from being my C.B.T. therapist, Alice is also my real estate broker. She was the one who sold us the land in The Springs in the first place.

Alice didn't start out as my real estate broker. At first she was just my C.B.T. therapist in New York City. But during one of our sessions, I told her we were going to rent a place at the beach for the weekend, and then she revealed that she had a weekend house right near the place we were renting. When I mentioned that I wanted to look at houses while we were out there, she told me that aside from being a C.B.T. therapist, she was also a real estate broker. She would be happy to take me around, she said.

After that, whenever we went out to the beach, even if it was just for a couple of days in a little weekend rental, I called her and asked her to take me around to look at places for sale. I'll admit, this was a little dishonest. I had no intention of buying a beach house. For one thing, we still had the lake house. But even after we sold the lake house, the houses in this area were too expensive for us. We could rent a low-budget one for a week or so, and that was about it.

I did not tell this to Alice, though. Instead, I told myself something else, which was that Alice and I were practically friends and that she really enjoyed hauling me around in her black sedan for an afternoon or two each summer to look at beach houses without my making a bid on anything.

It's really unbelievable what you can tell yourself. Now, of course, I realize that Alice and I may have been friendly, and she was indeed trying to help my thoughts become more well-behaved, but Alice was also patient. She knew very well what she was doing all those sunny summer afternoons, helping me cuddle beach houses for free.

Because finally one day, in the dead of winter, when I was in the city thinking that summer would never freaking come, she struck. She sent me an all-caps email that read SOMETHING REALLY AMAZING had come on the market that I should see: a little triangle of land for sale in Crashing Sound.

And here's what I found out then: a piece of land with nothing on it is much less expensive than a piece of land with a house on it, especially if that land is not *on* the water, but merely near it. This land, in fact, cost almost exactly as much money as we had made from selling our lake house.

I had never thought of looking at land before, because land was lacking the main thing I was interested in: a house. But now land seemed so exciting! So filled with possibilities!

I told George about the land, and we went out to see it without the kids so we could "focus," and we ended up buying it after seeing it in the snow, which was basically like not seeing it at all, and then when summer came and we saw it in its full flower, we realized it was not only shaped like a triangle, it sloped downward at a rather steep angle and was full of giant rocks. Plus, it was infested with deer ticks that could bite us and make us sick.

George started calling our land the tick farm. We were very good tick farm owners. We made a pilgrimage to our tick farm once each summer when we went out to The Springs to stay at a little rental house I had dubbed Chez Craigslist because that's where I found it. And George and the kids and I sat in the rental minivan and surveyed our tick farm and cheered and screamed, like we were watching a soccer game and our tick farm was about to score. We didn't actually get out of the car and walk around our tick farm, because of the ticks. But we loved it intensely from the car. We had many plans for what we would put on it, including installing some Twix-shaped topiary and a crow's nest on top of whatever structure we built. And this crow's nest would include a zip line that would let you sail down—naked!—into the pool.

Having a bit of land and imagining the house we wanted to put on it was very different from the experience of owning a house. We had bought the house on the lake after a friend of ours in the city had taken us up to the lake as his guests. We saw a house for sale while we were there for what we thought was a reasonable price— reasonable as long as we weren't thinking of upgrading our city apartment, that is. So we bought it without fussing over it, and then we didn't do a thing to it. We just accepted it as it was, with its one tiny bathroom, its potato-print wallpaper, and its wonky kitchen appliances from the 1970s. I loved the lake house, I really did. Until that raccoon came down the chimney like a demented Santa and haunted it in his bloody rampage.

Alice and I were in my therapy appointment. She wanted to talk about Bea's email. "It doesn't matter what kind of house it is—she can't dismiss it like that," Alice said testily. "That's the committee's job."

"What committee?"

If Alice was fiddling with her necklace, I couldn't tell. We had gotten to the point in my therapy where we didn't always use the camera. She was talking to me on speaker as she drove around between open houses.

"The Silver Sound Home Aesthetics Committee," she said. "They're supposed to approve all the building plans in your neighborhood. Just let Bea know that you know about it. That will be enough for her to understand that she has to have the house reviewed through the legitimate channels. She can't just tell you *no*."

"OK," I said wearily, hearing another job in the making.

"Of course," she added, "then you'll have to deal with the committee. Is your architect a people person?"

"Our architect is a character," I said.

9

FINDING THE RIGHT architect was surprisingly similar to finding the right wildlife control person. I just had to call the wrong person before I called the right one.

I called the first architect after we had had the tick farm for a full year. We had spent all our lake house money on the tick farm, and more money for a tick farm house was very annoyingly not falling on us from the sky.

At this point, you might ask me, well, why didn't *you* go out and make more money for a beach house if you wanted one so badly? This is a good question. And the answer is simple: because I knew I would never make enough. I was an English major, just like George. But I knew I would never "Hello?" my way into a lucrative career like he had. Oh sure, I had ambition once, right after I graduated from college. I had dreams of being an author. But I quickly found out that writing stories on the couch wasn't going to pay my phone bill. So I got a series of low-stress jobs tutoring or working at the bookstore, and I figured I would just do those jobs, or a combination thereof, forever, and I would survive.

And whether you said it was because I was scared, or I was lazy, or my relationship with money was all screwed up, the fact was, after I married George and had kids, I was very busy with all my not-real jobs, and George made enough money to support us. It seemed like this structure worked for us. So I thought, the hell with it.

And yet, I really wanted a beach house. This was crazy, I knew. And it was especially crazy because I had zero experience with beach house ownership. But I talked about it with my C.B.T. therapist/real estate broker, and *she* didn't think it was crazy. She framed it as part of a larger conversation we were having about what it means to be alive. I used to think aliveness was a binary: a person was either alive or dead. But now I know that aliveness is more like something on a continuum, like the pain scale. And I want to be more alive. I want to be as alive as possible. My beach house would help me do that. At my beach house I would get away from everything stressful in my life. I would stare at the heated pool and let all the suffering in the world go. I would zone out in my padded deck chair in my very own backyard: fully alive!

I then had another thought that seemed exceptionally brilliant: maybe we could just put something really inexpensive on our tick farm, like a port-a-potty next to a yurt. I would not have the heated pool or the padded deck chair, but I could make a start in their direction.

I did not tell George this thought. I didn't even tell Alice. I just barreled ahead and called this architect's office—he was a really fancy architect whose work I had admired online—and told the receptionist that I wanted to talk to the architect about putting something up on our land. I did not say what that something was. The receptionist asked me for the address of our land, and I told it to her, and she said she'd have the architect call me back.

The architect called me back a couple of days later when I was walking around the marble palace of the Deutsche Bank Center, on

West Fifty-Eighth Street. When my device buzzed, I was looking into a store window at a crystal-covered purse shaped like an owl. The architect and I said our hellos, and then the very first question he asked me was how much I wanted to spend on our beach house. This surprised me because I thought we were going to talk about houses and styles of houses—I could talk about those all day—and not prices.

But no, he wanted a price. He wanted me to say an actual number of dollars. And I did not have an answer for this, or at least I did not have an answer I could tell him, because the actual number was zero.

I said to him that George and I were still discussing it, which was obviously a stalling tactic. And then he said, "Well, you wouldn't want to spend less than X," and X was a really exorbitant number that consisted of many numbers in a row. But he said that was the number that would put our house in line with all the other houses in Crashing Sound, and he knew it because he had looked up the address of our land and done the research about housing prices in the area before he called me.

That's when I knew that this architect wasn't going to work for us because our goals were fundamentally opposed. This architect wanted us to put up a house that would have a price that was in tune with all the other houses' prices. The goal, as far as he was concerned, was having all the prices in harmony, so the prices would make a choir that would sing many beautiful money hymns.

That is not what I wanted at all. I did not care about singing the same money song as all the other houses in the neighborhood. I was in the area at all only by some crazy break in the universal fabric, like a raccoon who had fallen down a chimney.

I mean, yes, sure, we were there as legitimate tick farm landowners. But as far as this architect and his conversation with me went, we were not rich people who wanted to be like other rich people.

We were crazy people, and by "we," I mean me, the one in my marriage who has the most not-real job, makes the most no-money, and has the most rabid desire for a beach house.

But now that I think about it, I wish, when he had said, "Well, you wouldn't want to spend less than X," I had asked him: Why? Why wouldn't you want to use a different number? Is it because the architect wouldn't want to be paid less money? If so, fine—he could tell me that, and that would be good to know. He is free to set his price as he sees fit. But to put it on me, to act as if *I* wouldn't want to do that, because *I* wouldn't want to be different? I wish I had made him say that, in words. I wish I had made him say any of the things that get said, one way or another, in affordable-housing meetings, that if you are going to build a home that is worth less than all the homes around you, you are not adding value to the neighborhood. You are coming from somewhere else, with your different house, with its different numbers, and your numbers are dragging everyone else's numbers down. It's not personal, it's just numbers: clean, cold numbers, like figure eights into infinity. And what all those numbers always have to say is: get out.

I didn't try to have that conversation. I just finished talking with the architect and then kept walking around the marble mall. There was music in the mall, a pop song about wanting sex, but the song had been stripped of any voices, so you didn't hear the begging words. It was just an innocuous tune. You might not even know it was about begging at all, in fact.

As I walked around the mall and saw all the shiny things to buy, I felt bad about myself, like the problem was me, and my having no money, which I know is ridiculous. But still, I felt bad, like Oliver Twist, like I had said I wanted more, and I had been shamed for it.

10

I STARTED SEARCHING ONLINE for "cheap houses" and that's how I ended up calling Marianne, our architect. I got really excited when I found her because her site advertised that she could make a house that was one-fourteenth—1/14th!!—the price the first architect quoted me. The only hitch was that the house would be made out of used shipping containers. I did not see that as any kind of drawback. It was certainly a step up from a port-a-potty next to a yurt.

I was so pumped up that I thought I needed to calm myself down before I called her, so I decided to sit down and cuddle the dog.

I scratched Twix behind the ears, and rubbed her tummy, and set her back down on her sheepskin. And then I called the shipping container architect. She was out, so I left her a message, and then she called me back a few minutes later, which I thought was a good first sign.

I asked her right off if she could really make a house for that cheap, and she laughed and said, "Of course." And then we didn't talk about money anymore, which was a big relief after the first architect. We talked a little about the shipping containers and she explained that they came from all over the world and would have already crossed the ocean once when we bought them, and that's why they were so inexpensive: they were used. It was like we were getting them at the shipping container Salvation Army. After they landed somewhere stateside, they would get trucked up to a warehouse in Vermont where the architect had contracted workers who would trick them out with windows and walls and floors. And then finally they would get driven down to our site on several flatbed trucks, with escorts, and when she said that, I was picturing them being driven down with the *other* kind of escorts, and I smiled. This was my kind of architect!

Everything about the idea appealed to me. Turning these shipping containers into our home would be the right kind of acquisition narrative. It could serve as a correction for how we got our dog. We would rescue the containers from their terrible childhood, and then we would take them to the beach to retire. We would give our shipping containers a forever home by—how genius was this?!—turning them into a forever home. I'm not sure what the dog equivalent is there. Giving a dog a forever home by turning it into a taxidermy dog, maybe.

It would make a good story, and we could tell it to all our raccoon friends, who had shamed us about our failure to buy our dog correctly. So George and I met Marianne, a Black woman who was a little younger than us, in her thirties. She was strikingly beautiful, with a shaved head and bright red lipstick. We met her in person, at a café that was in between George's office and her office, and we had a coffee together and decided that we liked each other, and that it was OK to go ahead.

Winter

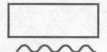

1

I DO NOT LIKE my own suffering, and I do not like anyone else's suffering. I just don't like any suffering at all. I would never make a good Mother Teresa.

I looked at my vision board. I was starting to accumulate some images. The pictures were mostly of swimming pools, which do not suffer, or at least I don't think they do.

I heard the door rattle, and Darby walked in with her multiple hoodie-hoods pulled up over her head, like she was trying to hide in there. She was eating a Vulnerability bar. I'd had one of those before. Never again.

As she picked up Twix, I caught a glimpse of the braided leather belt she was wearing with her jeans. Leather class must be going pretty well, I thought.

My phone buzzed. It was our real estate lawyer calling me back. His name was Tim, like my Atlantis-dwelling sea lion friend. Our lawyer Tim was unlike a sea lion, though, in that he was six four and ripped. When he wasn't lawyering, he was studying to be a shaman.

"Ah, those housing associations," Tim huffed dismissively, after I told him about Bea's email. "A bunch of cranks. They should all be doing more volunteer work."

"But isn't housing association work volunteer work?" I asked. "Those people aren't paid, are they?"

"They're not paid, but there are other perks," he said. "It's not *real* volunteer work, like feeding the unhoused."

I didn't want to tell Tim that I had once tried to sign us up to volunteer at a soup kitchen near our place on West Twenty-Seventh Street. I was put on a wait list, after which my neighbor Philip cracked that of course I was put on a wait list, because you couldn't get in there unless you knew someone. That particular soup kitchen, Philip told me, was "very cliquey."

Tim sounded winded, like he might be doing crunches. Tim knew Crashing Sound because he, like Alice, had a house nearby in The Springs, in addition to his place in the city.

"So what should I do?" I asked.

"Well, I know they can't sue," he declared. "They have no money. I say do whatever you want."

I told him Alice's advice about the committee.

"Yeah, do that, Shelly," Tim said, with a grunt. He paused, then added, "It'll all work out."

I hung up and wondered how much that forty-nine-second bit of reassurance cost me.

I wrote Bea an email in which I thanked her for her thoughtful response about our house and then said that George and I looked forward to speaking about it to the Silver Sound Home Aesthetics Committee. And then I added a smile emoji.

2

I DIDN'T HEAR FROM Bea for a few weeks, and I was starting to think that maybe she was going to leave us alone. I remembered the one time I had met her, when I was driving around looking at houses with Alice. Bea had been walking her Goldendoodle, and Alice had stopped the car to say hello. Alice was the sort of C.B.T.-certified real estate broker who knew everyone in town. Bea had seemed red-faced and agitated even then, and that was way before she knew about the tin can. But maybe she had calmed down now, I thought.

As soon as I dared hope that, of course, there she was, the next morning, in my inbox:

Dear Mr. and Mrs. Means, The Silver Sound Home Aesthetics Committee is looking forward to reviewing your plans.

She had written as if she herself were the committee, which maybe she was. She then listed the documents she wanted me to gather for her, including blueprints from the architect, a land survey from the surveyor, and proposed plans for the pool, septic tank, and well. I could see that this would be another new job for me, which was why, after I read the email, I hurled my bottle of raspberry-flavored Decency water against the couch.

I don't want any more jobs, I thought, as I went to perform another aspect of my taking-care-of-children job, which was packing a lunch for Clementine. Every weekday morning, I place this lunch in her brightly colored, waterproof lunch box, which is practically indestructible and would probably make a fine beach house if someone would just enlarge it a bit.

The problem with this particular job is that my limited cooking skills and Clementine's dislike of most foods are at an impasse. I have asked Clementine a hundred times what I should make her for lunch, but she won't tell me because she doesn't want anything I make. She wants ten identical cookies manufactured by the famous American multinational confectionery company. But she knows I won't pack those for her, which is how her lunch box has become a perfectly closed system of her wanting from me, and my not-giving to her, and my wanting from her, and her not-giving to me.

Part of the problem here is that Clementine likes order. She is obsessed with warding off sudden and unexpected disaster. She began to read early, at age three, and while George and I were thrilled at her precociousness and harbored dreams that she, too, might want to study the great works of literature, we were dismayed at what she gravitated to when she began reading on her own. She spent a solid month obsessed with a nonfiction book she pulled off Jack's shelf about JFK's assassination. When she applied for Chase, in kindergarten, we tried to brush it off during her interview when she made a block structure that she called "the book depository."

As part of this penchant, Clementine wants to eat manufactured food that is always the same taste and texture. She does not want any surprises in her mouth. This is why she will not eat the gourmet lunch at Chase, which boasts a cafeteria that routinely serves broiled salmon and mushroom risotto. I understand her perspective, but still, I struggle to feed her, because I am not a great cook in the first place and my food, when I do make it, definitely looks like what you could call "homemade."

I need Clementine to eat lunch at school so she doesn't pass out, though, so I don't put anything too homemade in it. I think of what I am doing when I make her lunch as a type of food collage. I assemble things made by others, kind of like building a beach house out of shipping containers. This is still a valid way of lunch making, I tell myself.

Here is what I put in her lunch: cheese and crackers, which she tells me she gives to her friend Katie; a Caring bar, which she eats because I started to buy the ones that have chocolate chips in them; and a milk box, which I know is terrible for the environment and I feel bad about that, but at least I know she will drink milk if it's in there. I also put in a fruit and/or vegetable to show her those things exist.

When she comes home, the cheese and crackers, milk box, and bar are gone. The fruit and/or vegetable come back. I regard the fruit and/or vegetable for the second time in a day. They are there for me, morning and evening, like prayer.

"You're so crabby these days," George said to me that evening, as I was contemplating the same three baby carrots in a snack bag that I had sent away that morning.

"I think I need to lie down," I said.

I lay down on our bed and thought about George and our children and Twix and how I cared for them and worried about them and advocated for them and comforted them and made them lunch they didn't eat and did all sorts of other stuff for them all day long. I knew I loved them, in fact, because I did these things.

I had a theory that whether or not I "loved" my family didn't matter, anyway, because people were as messed up about love as they were about money, probably more so. I had seen many mothers—my own mother as well as Mother Teresa—do all kinds of awful things in the name of their so-called love. What mattered, I had come to believe, was not whether I felt loving feelings when I dealt with my family. My feelings didn't matter; my actions mattered. And the actions that really counted most were the helping ones, and I did as many of those as I could.

I comforted myself with this idea as I lay on our bed with Twix, who adopted the position she takes when she sleeps: she lies on top of and behind my head, like my head is a faucet and she is the backsplash.

If you had told me, before I got a dog, that this is what my dog would do, I would not have believed it. My childhood dog slept in a cardboard box in the kitchen. That was just another grim fact of her life. We bought two beds for Twix, but she won't sleep in either of them. During the day she naps on her snack, the sheepskin rug, and at night, she sleeps in our bed, on my head. She is my furry sleep helmet, protecting me, even in my dreams.

With Twix backsplashing over my head, I thought, I am helping my children. Every day, I help them. Every day, I focus on my actions, and I try to do the right ones. I accept who my children are, and try to honor them, and help them get what they want, unless what they want is destructive and/or dumb and/or a dog, which I now know they were right about all along and I was wrong about, and now I missed all those dog years with my family and I hate myself.

And then, when I was already feeling bad, I spiraled further down and lost my ability to tell myself that my thoughts were just cognitive distortions, and I remembered The Incident in bold detail. I saw Kevin, the school board president/finance bro, telling us from behind a lectern in the conference room that we were failing our children, and there was a big problem at our school, and the problem was that it didn't have a financial literacy curriculum.

And guess which investment services company offered one of those? The one he worked for, Cash Winehouse. And Cash Winehouse, he told us, would be happy to offer their curriculum to our school at a discount, and his nephew Josh could come in and teach it, and Josh would be accompanied by a special guest the kids would go crazy over, which was Cashy, the Cash Winehouse Financial Literacy Robot, who made learning about technology and finances fun. The robot did this by playing financial literacy games with the kids and then giving the winners Cash Winehouse wristbands like the ones he had so generously brought for us that evening. Please, go ahead, take one.

But wait, there's more, he might as well have said, as he told us about Cash Winehouse's investment planning services, which Josh could also tell us about at our next board meeting. Josh could even bring Cashy to that, too, if we wanted.

I sat there, blinking and feeling my face get hot, and then I broke the rule I had told myself I was going to abide by during this meeting, which was that I wasn't going to say anything, because I hadn't been doing this PTA gig very long and I was watching Sharon, another no-real-work mom like me, to figure out how to conduct myself. And that just shows you how desperate I was, because Sharon was the kind of hypercompetitive mom who makes her kids' Halloween costumes *at* you.

And finally I couldn't hold it in anymore, and I opened my mouth, and once that happens, all bets are off because my thoughts and my mouth are very closely connected, and my thoughts, as you know, are still not fully trained.

I told Kevin that I thought that his proposals were inappropriate and that he shouldn't be taking advantage of his position to sell his company's products to our children, let alone to us.

You would have thought I was saying something really outlandish, because the other parents stared me down after I said that, and one of them, Kevin's finance-bro friend, told me that I was being "very petty," because Kevin had "done" so much for our school, and by "done" he meant that Kevin had donated major cheddar. And then more parents who had real jobs in high-rise buildings in Midtown piled on and agreed with him, and I felt rage starting to come out of my eyes in liquid form, and a frog hopping around in my throat, and nurse sharks in my heart, as if my body were an Atlantis with animals cavorting inside it. And I was ashamed that this was happening without my wanting it to, and then I threw, as I told you, my fancy new water bottle in the general direction of Kevin and his stupid, Cashy-loving head.

Thank god that that bottle didn't hit Kevin, or anyone else, and merely plonged against the opposite wall of the conference room and made a dent in the wall. But the greater damage was done, and I had to be escorted out of the meeting by the school security guard, Jeff, who was someone I really liked and had said good morning to for years, and Jeff's holding me by the elbow and essentially tossing me out the front door as he shook his curly-haired head and refused to meet my gaze was the humiliation cherry on top of the shame sundae I had already made for myself at the mortification ice cream bar of this PTA meeting.

The next day Kevin wrote an email demanding that I step down from my PTA position or I would be fired from it, and that's when George said I had to choose between anger-management classes or therapy.

Remembering all this made me feel like a little child in my own bed, a child who was suffering, and I had no real, live mother who could help me. Although Twix did lick my face because I had put face cream on it and she thinks my face cream is delicious.

I sighed and pulled up my internal mother so I could tell my internal child that mistakes are how we learn. And then I thought, Good god, when will I figure out how to get along in this world, until eventually I left it for a few hours and slept.

3

THE NEXT MORNING I texted my friend Walter, a painter I had met years ago when I was working at the bookstore. He was one of my few artist friends. He was really successful now. His work sold at auction for crazy money.

I want to be a terrible person, I texted him.

You? Hahahaha, he replied.

I understood what he was saying. I probably seem like a pretty upstanding individual, even if you count The Incident, and that only happened once.

Why do you want to be a terrible person? he continued.

I'm tired of trying to do the right thing all the time. It's exhausting and I keep screwing it up.

Well, get out there and try doing the wrong thing, he offered.

But that's even more exhausting. Plus it's anxiety-provoking.

I saw the little bubbles forming on the screen like he was going to reply, but then he didn't.

What are you working on? I asked.

He sent me a photo of a painting. Walter painted objects that were already recognized as desirable. That way the irresistibility of the paintings was built-in, he explained. I studied the image. It was a luscious-looking cheeseburger.

Varnishing the cheeseburger! he wrote.

I read "varnishing" as "vanishing." Vanishing the cheeseburger didn't seem like an odd thing for Walter to be doing. He was a bit of a magician.

I put a heart on his cheeseburger. Have you been reading much lately? We liked to talk about books.

Literary fiction. There isn't much wrongdoing in it tho. Only trauma and disaster.

Maybe that's why it doesn't sell, I wrote.

Walter put a heart on that.

4

I WAS SITTING IN Clementine's tiny bedroom, on her bed. Jerry, our cleaning person, was cleaning the living room. I had gone into Clementine's room to get out of Jerry's way. Clementine was in the bathroom. She had the sniffles and was home from school.

Having a cleaning person work for me is something that I have only had as an adult. We never had any helpers like that growing up, and I didn't know anyone who did. When I think about my friends' houses from when I was a kid, I see now that they were all really messy. People just threw crap everywhere. Now the richer people are, it seems, the more their houses are empty. Our apartment is messy in the way that my friends' houses were when I was young, but this is because George is a borderline hoarder and not because Jerry does not do a good job.

Clementine came in. "You're in my room," she declared accusingly.

"I'm staying out of Jerry's way," I explained.

She wiped her nose with the sleeve of her nightgown as she got back into bed and eyed the Pantone chip I was holding. "What's that?"

"I'm trying to decide what color to paint our beach house," I said. I looked at the Pantone chip, Punch. Did I want a punch house?

"Oh, simple," Clementine said. "Black."

I looked down at Clementine, who wore her pink nightgown under a pink blanket in her pink-walled bedroom. "Your room's not black," I said.

"You wouldn't let me paint it black," she said evenly. "I did ask you."

I didn't remember telling her that. "You like pink, though, don't you?"

"I like it OK, but black is better," she said, as she opened a book about Chernobyl.

Jerry popped his head in. "Done!" he said, hooking his thumb toward the living room. Jerry had his earbuds in. He was an aspiring actor who lived in Queens. I hired him through a cleaning service that said they used only organic cleaning products. I worried about chemicals.

I left Clementine in bed, looking at pictures of reactors. I didn't want her to be a weirdo like I had been when I was a kid, but it was probably too late. I hoped she would be reasonable about money. They say kids get their understanding through what you do, not what you say.

I sat in the living room with Twix and remembered how, on the way home from that family trip to the Black Hills, we stopped at the famous Wall Drug, in South Dakota. In a moment of what might have been sympathy but was probably more like exhaustion, my mother had veered from her usual stance regarding trinket buying and said I could get *one* thing. She said that so seldom that I became very anxious trying to decide what to buy because I didn't want to make a mistake and get something that would disappoint me. I kept thinking the problem was me and my poor choices, and not what the world, on all its display shelves, had to offer me.

And just to show you how determined I was not to screw this up, how really hell-bent I was on making a good decision, and not choosing something that would break immediately, or have a piece snap off, or need some special batteries we could never find, here is what I finally chose to buy: a bag of rocks. The sign beside them said they were small bits of turquoise that came from deep inside the earth of the Black Hills themselves. I carried this little white linen bag to the counter with the money my mother had given me, and I bought the rocks and carried the rocks in my right front pants pocket for the remainder of the trip. This bag of rocks was something from the world under the earth. It was not from the world on top of the earth, the one we were so grimly driving through at a beer-fueled eighty miles an hour. Knowing that I had something from that underground otherworld helped me as I sat in the car, where my father's hangover burps were emerging from caverns deep inside his body and hovering thickly in the air.

It was late at night when we arrived home, and I was half-asleep when I took my clothes off and put them in the hamper. I had forgotten that my pants contained my treasure, which is how I found out, after my mother did the laundry, that the turquoise and my rocks were two separate things. The turquoise on my rocks had been applied with paint. The washing machine had transformed my magic bag of turquoise rocks into a bag of plain white rocks indistinguishable from the gravel in our driveway.

My parents and my sister laughed at me when I told them this. Later, when I was alone, I dumped those lying, duplicitous rocks in the driveway. I dumped them on a spot where I knew my father's compact car would efficiently roll over them, backward and forward unrelentingly, like machines do in hell.

I'm doing OK with how I handle money in front of Clementine and Jack, I assured myself. I never wanted to *talk* about money, but I thought I was doing OK with how I was handling it. Our bills were paid. We had a tax guy named Ricky, and once a year we threw all our receipts at him and he filled out all our forms and kept us out of trouble. And most important of all, I thought, we didn't buy crazy-expensive things we couldn't afford, except just this once, now, with this beach house.

Clementine would say that her mother is responsible with money, I thought. I mean, *I* know I'm not good with money. Wait, that's not right: I am OK with money. I am just not good at *making* money. I am good at spending money. I am good at buying groceries and paying bills. I am good at stamping envelopes with checks in them and putting them in the mail. I am good at paying bills electronically. I can do lots of things with money when it is already there.

But I am not as good as I could be. For example, I don't balance our checkbook; I just record my deposits and withdrawals haphazardly and hope it all evens out. Maybe you don't even need to do that balancing business anymore; maybe robots do that. I remember when I was a kid, my father used to lose his mind once a month when he could not get his checkbook to balance. He spent hours in his study, swearing and drinking beer and occasionally throwing things—he once broke the pinch-pot ashtray I made him by hurling it at the door—until he could finally get all the numbers to line up how he wanted them.

It's my job to handle our family's checkbook now, and under my expert management, it works like this: I write the checks, either on real paper or electronically, and I record the numbers and keep a tally of them when I remember, which is about half the time. And when I write checks for really big bills, like for an architect who designs discount beach houses, I write it off a savings account we have for big bills, and I ask George first, can we cover this? And he almost always says yes, but sometimes he says no, just wait a couple of days, and I wait, and while I am waiting he moves money from one place to another, and I could ask him more about that, but instead I imagine him wearing a cowboy hat and a bandanna over his face and venturing into some dark, dusty cave, and in the back of the cave there are gleaming gold bars and he moves the bars around in different pyramid-type configurations and it's kind of spooky in there and also maybe there are bears, and I am not sure I want to know anything else about what happens in that place. I just wait for him to do that work, and I don't look at it, like when I wait for the wildlife control people to call and tell me what's happening with my raccoon.

And then once George finishes in the cave and tells me OK, I write the check, meaning, I write the numbers on the pale green paper rectangle in two ways, first as numbers $123, and then as words, one hundred twenty-three dollars, and then I sign my name, Shelly Means, and in that moment, I am as real as I will ever be in the world.

I can do all that, but I can't make money appear. I'm like one of those guys in the city who runs a shell game on a cardboard box. I can move around the money very well. I just can't supply it, is all.

This is something I am ashamed about, especially in regard to my daughter, because I want her to see me as someone who is capable of making money in a "real" job. But so far I can't figure out how to do that except in this unreal job where I do a billion tasks a day (except clean the apartment) and still, I am viewed as not working.

I also can't hide the fact that I don't know very much about, say, complex securities. It's not anything I would admit to the PTA at my kids' fancy school, but I'm probably not even financially literate.

I would have been much better off availing myself of Cashy-the-robot's financial literacy curriculum than throwing water bottles at Kevin's head.

This is why I keep our money in its proper place, out of my mind, like horrible suffering. I respect it and keep it at a distance, and don't look at it directly in its terrible face. And that way, I think, I am protected: I can handle money.

Jerry finished cleaning and left, and then George came home. And when George came in the door, he looked at me and said, "Shelly, this is serious. We have to stop spending so much."

5

I DIDN'T REALLY UNDERSTAND what my father's job was, when I was a kid. My father said he did purchasing for companies, but I did not understand why companies needed to buy anything. I thought the point of a company was to sell things, and that's how they made money.

My father's company was a big company that owned many other smaller companies that sold things. And as it turned out, my father was responsible for purchasing, for all these smaller companies, the tissue-thin plastic bags that we now know are doing terrible damage to the earth and are outlawed in many states. He was an early adopter of them.

I am a tiny bit glad my father is buried in the earth now and not walking around on top of it, because I know if he saw this development, he would feel really bad about it.

You will note that this job of my father's does not sound like a working-class job. And it is true that my father sat at a desk and was an executive. But the way he handled money was in the manner of someone who didn't have much of it. It did not matter how much of it he bagged, nor how much the bags weighed. The numbers were never big enough for him.

My mother outlived my father by many years. Thanks to his bags of money, she was able to spend the last twenty years of her life in an assisted-living place in Florida that some marketing genius named Hamptons Woods. She had a roommate toward the end who was older than she was, and this new roommate didn't have to use a wheelchair. My mother had to use a wheelchair all the time, so she was envious. My mother found a way to spin her situation, though. She reframed her wheelchair as a prize she had won. That was why she had it and that was why she had to use it, she told anyone who would listen: she had been awarded it.

I admired this change in her narrative, and I have now found a way to use this approach myself, on our family expenditures. This is how I do it: I think, I am so grateful that I have this partner and two children and a dog who need stuff all the time, because I pay for everything we need with my credit card, and my credit card gives me rewards. I am not spending money when I buy things. I do not have a certain amount of money and then I buy things and then I have less money. No, when I use my credit card, I am earning rewards.

The really great thing about this is that our credit card is hooked up to a company that owns hotels, so the thing I am rewarded with is hotel rooms, which is truly the best, PhD-level, wildlife-control-person reward for me. This is why George and I have a date night on as many nights as we can arrange it: so we can visit free hotel rooms.

That I have figured this out about money, all by myself, without George's search engine brain or any financial literacy robot named Cashy helping me—well, it feels amazing, like I have finally conquered middle school algebra, like I understand how those hedge fund guys feel, moving money around so it has sex with itself and makes more money. I feel fantastic every time I get our credit card statement.

Or this was how I used to feel, before George said we had to start watching our expenses.

I know it's not really admirable to say this, but when I feel guilty about buying so much crap that people suffered to make, in really appalling working conditions, so that I might earn free hotel rooms, here is what I do: I try to keep the whole situation out of my head. But sometimes it finds a way in, so that when George and I go to our rewarding hotel room, I feel a tiny bit of horror in the pleasure, as I roll around on the king bed and scream.

WHEN GEORGE TOLD me that we had to stop spending money, I asked him why, and he said his agent told him that what he had predicted was, in fact, true: he had screwed up the chicken sandwich recording session with his inability to articulate the wry twist. And now, just as he had anticipated, the word was out that he couldn't voice sandwiches, which meant he would never voice cars.

No calls were coming in. "Zero," his agent had told him, not putting a wry twist on that number at all.

I wasn't sure what to say. I didn't think I spent that much money. The only thing I wanted that cost money, I thought, was a beach house. And that was only one thing. One!

I told George that we would stop spending so much money and then he hugged me and we stopped talking about it and I thought we were done with that discussion.

But then Marianne called and said she wanted me and George to come to her office and talk about house design. This would have been a good time for me to say, you know, Marianne, we've had some financial setbacks and we can't go ahead with the plans right now.

But I couldn't bring myself to say that. Instead, I set a date to meet Marianne and figured I would just go by myself. I didn't want to go without telling George, though, because that would be too sneaky. But I waited for the right moment to broach it with him.

I waited until we were lying in bed one night and he was researching the prices of obscure vintage soccer jerseys because he had just found one at a thrift store for cheap. Twix was on my head. I reached up to pet her, and she licked my hand. Then I took a breath.

"We have a meeting with Marianne coming up," I said.

"We can't go forward with that now," George replied, not lifting his eyes from the screen.

"It's only been a month since the sandwich gig," I pleaded, looking at him. "Something else will come up."

He put down his device and regarded me squarely. "You don't understand. It's a different world for me now. My voice can't sell anything."

I sat up. "Well, shouldn't you be looking for other work, then?"

As soon as I said that, I knew I shouldn't have.

"What do you think I'm doing?" he shot back.

I lay back down. "Maybe we should just sell the land," I said. I was hoping he would say no, of course we shouldn't do that.

"We should definitely do that," he said, returning to his device. "You should call Alice about it tomorrow."

7

THE NEXT MORNING I woke up and asked myself, what would my mother do, if she were faced with having to sell her prize beach house before she even got it? I put my hair up in a ponytail and tried to figure it out.

When I was growing up, my mother used to use our dishwasher as a bread box because she did not trust it. She called it an "energy waster" that "sucked money." She did all the dishes herself in a plastic tub she put in the sink, and then she let the dishes dry on dish towels she set on the counter beside the sink. She then put the plastic tub under the sink to store it. She was very particular about the condition of this plastic tub when it got put away under the sink. It had to be put away perfectly dry. If it was in any condition other than perfectly dry, it was a total failure, and I knew the depths of this failure because I was responsible for it many times.

Whenever we had cookies in our house—and we almost never had them because my mother was forever watching her weight—

they were carefully placed in the top rack of the dishwasher, where other people put their drinking glasses.

Jack was sitting next to me at the kitchen table in the apartment. We were having a leisurely Saturday, enjoying egg-and-cheese sandwiches from the deli on the corner where I had walked with Twix earlier in the morning.

Jack had always been pale, but now his pallor was accentuated by a black forelock that he occasionally shook out of his eyes. He looked like an anime character. He was a dutiful firstborn, taking his big-brother relationship to Clementine seriously and carrying on the frustrated dreams of his parents. He had already told me and George that he was an aspiring writer.

I gave Jack a very abbreviated and tame overview of our no-money situation and then asked him what he thought I should do about it.

"If you need money, you should write fiction," he counseled. "That's what Roberto Bolaño did after he had a family and wanted to make money: he turned to fiction."

I hadn't read any Bolaño. Jack pulled up something on his device and held it out to me. "Here," he said. "I was going to use this myself, but you can have it. It's an outline for a young adult novel. All you have to do is flesh it out."

I studied it. I knew he was trying to encourage me to pick up my old dream of writing. But I didn't want to tell him I didn't care about that anymore. I just wanted to lie around in my tin can and feel fully alive.

"This is what young adults want to read?" I asked him.

"This is what sells," he countered.

I stood up and went to the kitchen to get more coffee. It would be good for someone—not me, but someone—to write a novel that would sell well because novels that sell well have the best chance of being turned into movies, and a movie, let's face it, is the end-all. If you write something that manages to be watched on a screen, you have passed the sandwich-voice level and reached the car-voice level of what the written word can do. In terms of being lucrative, that is.

I knew there was no way I would ever write a YA novel. Too hard. I didn't want to admit that to my son, though. I had already spent so much of his childhood trying to sell him on the importance of trying and failing and trying again at something really difficult. Or, as Chase called it, grit.

8

THE WAY THAT George is always looking for junk reminds me of my mother, only my mother didn't look for castoffs in the street. She liked to look for treasure in the other outside: nature.

I was in elementary school the first time she drove me, one Saturday morning in summer, to a hiking trail near our house in Minneapolis. She parked the car and then told me to follow her down the trail. We came to a shallow creek, and then she took off her shoes and stepped in the water and told me to come in with her.

I had a hard time processing my mother's behavior. According to what I knew, my mother did the following: drove, cooked, cleaned, bought stuff, made holidays appear, worried about my father's drinking, moved papers around on her desk, and yelled. Nowhere in there was walking in creeks with no shoes on.

"We're looking for agates," she said.

The creek was cold, but it was shallow enough to be bearable in the sun. After twenty minutes of walking, bent over, picking up rocks and examining them, my mother let out a triumphant hoot and showed me what she had found: a rock with tiger stripes on its sides. She put it in my palm. "Agate," she said.

We spent several weekend days that summer looking for agates in the creek. Both of us looked for them, but it was mostly my mother who found them. The few that I found, I treasured. They were visible signs that I, too, could find something valuable in the world, if only I was patient and looked carefully. Whether my mother planned this consciously or not, this activity helped me rebuild my consumer confidence after having been duped at Wall Drug. Maybe I could discern when a rock had value, after all.

My mother was so enamored of our rocks that she bought a rock polisher. The rock polisher lived in the laundry room in the basement, across the hall from my bedroom. It made a noise like the washing machine on steroids. I couldn't believe how long it took to polish a rock: three solid days.

When I first saw my agates after they had been polished, I was surprised. I had thought they would emerge from the tumbler somehow larger and more sparkly, but instead they seemed smaller, like sweaters that had shrunk in the dryer. They were silkier, though. They were like minuscule, striped kittens I held in my palm. I kept them in a special ceramic box shaped like a dachshund that I had lined with a scrap of pink velvet. I didn't show them to anyone. I admired them when I was alone.

9

I COULD NOT SEE my way through to any other beach house acquisition strategies. I was totally frustrated. I felt like Rupert Murdoch when he was stonewalled in his takeover bid for Time Warner.

"We need to sell the land," I announced grimly to Alice, as I sat on the couch in the apartment on West Twenty-Seventh Street, having my on-screen therapy session. I had stopped being concerned about where my C.B.T. thought training ended and my real estate shenanigans began. It was all one big process of feel-better-now.

"Of course," she said briskly, because whether she is doing real estate or C.B.T., she is in the service industry. "But is there a particular reason? You didn't even get the house up."

"We don't have the money for it now," I said. It was hard to get those words out.

"Ah," she said. I sensed some concern on her part. Alice the C.B.T. therapist did not do sliding scale.

There was a pause as both of us sat there. We seemed to be observing my financial failure like it was a plastic dishpan that had been stored under the sink incorrectly.

"Well, it's up to you, of course," Alice said at last. "But I want to remind you that this house isn't really a purchase you're making. You know that, right?"

I did not know that. "Huh?"

"You aren't building a house near the beach," she explained patiently. "You're building a revenue stream."

"I don't get it, Alice," I said flatly.

She chuckled. "You have to remember that you're going to be able to sell this house for *a lot* more than it cost to build. It's in such a desirable area!"

"Do you really think so?" I asked. Crashing Sound was nice and all, and *I* certainly liked it, but there were a couple of streets that George and I referred to as "Lower Crashing Sound," where the ground was kind of swampy, and there was a vacant lot where people surreptitiously took their flat-screen TVs to die.

"Of course! Plus, you know you can rent it out for the summer months, right? Do you know how lucrative that can be?"

"Really?"

"Absolutely!" she said.

I was grinning. How had I not realized this? I wasn't getting a house for myself, of course I wasn't! I was getting a house for *other people*. I would rent it out to them, and I would do it honestly, for a fair price. I was practically engaged in a public service!

"You're just overwhelmed by the building process," Alice said sympathetically. "Everyone gets overwhelmed when they build. It's a big job. Let's do some breathing."

I closed my eyes and inhaled.

"All is well," Alice intoned.

"All is well," I repeated.

"I radiate love," Alice said.

"I radiate love," I said. I inhaled, then exhaled, then opened my eyes.

Alice was looking at me. "Good," she said.

"I have so many jobs, Alice," I whined.

"Yeah, and now you're gonna have another one," she said, taking a sip of her chai. "Because you're going to stay on top of the contractor. They're inundated with work, and your low-price job won't be a priority for them."

"Perfect," I said, rolling my eyes.

10

Encouraged by my talk with Alice, I decided not to cancel the meeting with Marianne. I would just go to the meeting myself, without George. I wasn't being duplicitous, I reasoned. I would tell George all about it afterward, when I also explained about how our house wasn't just a house, it was a revenue stream.

I changed out of my everyday black sweatpants that had dog cookie crumbs ground into the pockets and put on my dress black sweatpants that had dog cookie crumbs ground into the pockets *and* a subtle black stripe down the side.

Marianne's office was what you might call minimal. There wasn't a receptionist. There wasn't a waiting area. It was just one big room with a conference table, chairs, several file cabinets, and Marianne.

"Sit down, sit down," she said, smiling, as I walked in. She looked dazzling, her long gold earrings swaying as she gestured for me to sit at a chair at the conference table. I glanced at her diploma on the wall: it was from Carnegie Mellon. She had large black-framed glasses on top of her head and wore an expensive-looking electric-blue pantsuit. I wished I had stepped it up a notch from dress sweatpants.

"Before we start talking about architecture, I want you to spend a minute and explore some configurations with these," she said, pushing a pile of silver-colored blocks toward me.

"You want me to play with blocks?" I asked.

"This isn't 'playing with blocks,'" she said sharply. "Part of my process of getting to know my clients is seeing what they do naturally with these forms."

I didn't say anything. But I thought: I have accompanied my kids to interviews at multiple New York City preschools. I know a block area when I see it.

These blocks had been made so an adult could play with them and not feel silly. They looked expensive. They didn't interlock, but you could stack them. They were proportionally the same size as shipping containers, Marianne told me. She'd had them custom made.

She was smart, this architect. I played with the expensive, custom-made blocks on a piece of paper she had put down that was a proportionally sized drawing of our tick farm. As I did this, Marianne brought me ice water in a wineglass. If she had brought me wine it would have been like we were at one of those drink-and-paint places where adults go to unleash their creativity.

Marianne sat beside me and took notes as I played. I became absorbed in the task. I soon discovered that our tick farm was such a small triangle that there was only one way you could position several shipping containers on it and still have room for a septic tank, and I very much wanted a septic tank so that my Japanese toilet could flush.

The most number of containers that we could fit on the land was four. Four was a good number. It was at least one number away from numbers 1 and 2.

Marianne was excited. "You've hit on a fantastic shape!" she said. "This is going to be amazing!"

I couldn't believe that I had found my beach house design in twelve minutes like I was solving a tangram puzzle at my preschool interview.

Marianne took her glasses off the top of her head and put them over her eyes. She looked at me through the lenses. "I've been looking at your list of must-have items for the house," she said. "And I feel like this would be a good time to have a reality check about what it is you want and what you said you wanted to spend. Unless that's changed," she added, fixing her gaze on me.

I sat there, like a rock.

"From what I see here," she continued, turning her screen to show me the list she had compiled, "you want four bedrooms, three bathrooms, a heated pool, heated floors, a basement, a garage, and some very high-end finishes and appliances."

I nodded. It sounded like I wanted so much.

"I'm afraid, given your budget, that you're going to have to cut some things. How important is the garage to you?"

"Not important," I said quickly, grateful that George wasn't in on this conversation. I watched her delete "two-car garage" from the list.

"We can give you a gravel driveway instead," she said. "Also, heated floors are prohibitively expensive. Are they deal-breakers?"

"No," I said, lying.

"Those need to go, too, then. And we may have to cut some more, depending on how far over budget we go."

"Of course," I said, feeling my stomach sink but trying to sound like a voice-over artist who could add a little smile to whatever she was saying.

11

A WEEK LATER, I was sitting in the kitchen, when the door rattled. I assumed it was Darby, but then remembered today was Saturday. I got up to get the door.

A purple-haired, brown-skinned teenage girl stood there, dressed in what looked like a black garbage bag.

"Hi?" I uptalked.

"I'm here for Jack," she said, as Jack rushed out from his tiny bedroom.

"Mom, this is Betty," he said, smiling as he ushered her in and put his arm around her. They looked googly-eyed at each other, then hugged.

I stared at them. I knew my high-school-aged son was going to have a love interest eventually. But I didn't think "eventually" meant *now*.

I studied Betty's outfit. Not only was she wearing a trash bag dress, but her feet were covered in the same thin plastic bags my dear dead dad had helped loose upon the world.

Betty noticed me looking. She flipped her violet hair. "These shoes are great, aren't they? They're Comme des Garçons."

"Betty is in my social studies class, Mom," Jack announced. "We're doing a group presentation on economic inequality."

I picked up my device in order to send George a picture of this new development: our son had a crush!

"The number of unhoused people in New York City is currently at unprecedented levels," Betty informed me.

I nodded. I had been reading a book about money, but it wasn't about economic inequality. It was called *Think Your Way Rich*, and it was a book of mantras that you were supposed to repeat every day in order to become wealthy. My favorite mantra in the book so far was "Only poor people see obstacles."

Betty and Jack disappeared into Jack's bedroom as I went to the kitchen, opened the refrigerator, and looked inside absently. Chase schooled their students carefully in the idea that having a lot of money wasn't normal, I had noticed. You could be a kid there who had a solid-gold private plane—the plane wasn't the problem. The problem was if you acted like it was *normal* to have a solid-gold private plane. You had to demonstrate that you understood that your access to your beautiful, sparkly plane was not a standard way of life—even if it was *your* standard way of life, and you flew in it to and from Chase every day.

This was probably why billionaires liked to hang around other billionaires in places like East Hampton, I reasoned. They didn't have to spend all that energy pretending. They could just sit behind their hedges together, pissed off about all their luxury problems.

12

I DECIDED TO TALK to George about the beach house after we did our annual trip to his mother's in January. Every year we drove a rental car up to his mom's house in Dorchester. She still lived there, in the same house George grew up in.

It was always the same itinerary. We arrived there in the evening, stayed over at a hotel, visited with her the next day, and then left the following morning. It was two days of getting to and from her house, and one day of actually being at her house. It was even less being at her house for George, because he generally did not hang around with Gina, his mom, so much as scour the Dorchester Salvation Armies.

Gina and I got along OK. She thought I was stupid, but I didn't take it personally. She had raised George as a single mother, and he was her golden only child. Yet somehow he had married me, a woman who didn't work and had anger issues besides.

George had taken Jack with him to check out Salvation Armies. Clementine was running around outside in the snowy backyard with Twix, pretending to be a member of the Donner Party.

Gina and I sat in her living room and watched a judge yell at a crying woman on the giant flat-screen George had bought her. I glanced around the living room at the framed demolition derby posters from the nearby Topsfield Fair where George had gone with his mother when he was a kid. My favorite was the bright yellow poster featuring cars crashing and the words ROAD RAGE ARAMA.

George burst in the door with Jack, holding a plastic bag aloft. "Score!" he cried. He pulled a yellow-and-pink plaid sweater out of the bag. You might charitably call it loud.

"I'm going to start flipping these," he said to his mother and me. "I must have ten of them now." He put the sweaters on the table and threw the plastic bag in the trash.

"Not so fast," Gina chided him, pulling the bag out of the garbage. "I can reuse that." Gina opened a drawer overflowing with plastic bags and shoved the newly rescued bag into it. "Have you been doing any voice-overs lately?" she asked George. She loved to hear him on her TV.

"I auditioned for one last week," he said.

I raised my eyebrows. This was news to me.

"I didn't want to get your hopes up," he said to me.

"What was it for?" Gina asked.

He put on his voice-over voice. "Feel better, faster," he said. "With Placatrex."

Gina laughed delightedly. George smiled.

"What's Placatrex?" I asked.

"Some drug for your stomach," he said.

"When do you know if you get the gig?" I asked.

"Maybe this week," he replied.

George always wrote his mother a check before we left. It was pretty much the only time he wrote a check himself. I think it was important to both of them that the check bore his signature and not mine.

The next morning, after George gave his mother the check, we headed back to the city. George was smiling and humming to Johnny Cash.

"I spoke with Alice about the land," I began.

George and Johnny were walking the line.

"She said we shouldn't view it as an expense because it's really an additional revenue stream," I continued.

"Hmm–mmm," George hummed.

"Let's at least see if the committee will approve it," I said, "and then we can decide whether to go forward from there."

"OK," he said.

I was quiet. I knew a score when I had it.

13

AS A VERY little kid, I liked to read *Aesop's Fables*. I think of them as the ancient Greek precursor to cat videos. What made the fables more than just cat videos, though, was the final line—the moral. The story would end with the dogs, frogs, and raccoons just sitting there, in the middle of whatever mess they had made, and then Aesop would abandon his narrator voice and come in and say something in his very own Aesop voice, and I felt like he spoke *to me*. It was like god himself had parted the clouds to give me advice.

Aesop's morals were important: they were centered on the page and/or in italics. They brought the story home, and made it personal, and gave me something to go out and do. They made it so I wasn't just reading an animal-behaving-badly story as a distraction, the way I now watch videos of cats breaking vases for fun. I was reading about terrible animal behavior in order to avoid going out and doing something terrible and animal myself.

I was grateful for this because everyone in my family acted like living was so easy. You just woke up and went about your business freezing your ass off, not trusting the dishwasher, and sampling dog cookies, and that's the way it was. I liked the idea that someone, anyone—even a pontificator who lived in ancient Greece and wrote about foxes and frogs, fine—was trying to help me out. Aesop, it seemed to me, would see something unsatisfactory in all this. And not only would he see it, he would try to help.

Sadly, it appears that Aesop himself learned very little from the stories of right conduct that he told throughout his life. He reportedly was thrown off a cliff by his neighbors for stealing a gold or silver cup.

If Aesop actually lived—there is some debate over whether he was truly alive or not, making him indeed a relatable narrator for me—it's like his own life needed nothing so much as an Aesop. It needed someone coming in at the end to make sense of it. But maybe that's what everybody's life needs.

14

I HAD GOTTEN A surveyor to come in and survey the land, which was exorbitant. And then Marianne had drawn up the house plans from the survey and sent me an invoice. It was a big invoice, so I asked George if we could cover those bills.

George was grouchy when he heard about the bills, but I reminded him what he had said: we should continue to walk the line with the beach house. He didn't say anything. But he wasn't high on writing checks to his mother anymore, and he wasn't happy about writing more checks to anyone else.

"If the committee says our house design won't work," he said to me, "we are going to stop this nonsense, sell the land, and get out of this beach house business."

I said nothing. I wrote the checks. Then I got busy mailing the papers, in triplicate, to Bea. She confirmed that she had received them and said that she would soon set a date for the meeting. By doing this she underscored our relative positions: she was the person doing the setting of dates, and I was the person waiting for dates to be set.

The meeting would include the three people on the committee, as well as Bea, Marianne, George, and me. It would take place in the clubhouse by the beach, which was a little hut that was too small to hold the housing association cocktail parties but big enough for a conference table and chairs, a refrigerator, and a bathroom. The bathroom was used by everyone when the cocktail parties were on the beach.

I told George about the meeting as he was headed out to an audition. He didn't seem fazed by the prospect. "Do I have to dress up?" he asked.

"Business casual should do it," I told him.

He kissed me and headed out the door. I had just put a picture of fluffy green beach towels on my vision board as I heard Darby walk in.

Today Darby's hoodie was a tie-dye number in bright yellow and orange. She didn't wear regular hoodies in single colors emblazoned with names of colleges or sports teams. All her hoodies advertised weird bands or obscure fashion labels. It was hard for me, as an always-cold person, to believe that she didn't need a Minneapolis-style parka in the winter, but all the dog walking kept her warm, she said.

Darby gazed at my vision board. It was starting to look a lot more visionary now. I had Pantone chips, swimming pool pictures, toilet pictures, and tile samples. It had taken a while to amass all that. In the beginning, when I first bought the corkboard, I thought I had a lot of vision. But it wasn't all that easy to fill those fuckers up, I had discovered.

"Why don't you have any pictures of your children on there?" she asked me.

"I do have pictures of my children. They're here," I said, gesturing to the coffee table with framed pictures. I didn't want to explain to her that I didn't need my children on my vision board because my vision board is supposed to help things become real and my children are already extremely real to me.

"Children are nice," she said, petting Twix.

"Children bear terrible burdens," I said, thinking of Clementine, who called every day she spent at her fancy school with its elegant lunch "forced labor."

"I think you need a vacation," she said.

That was kind of a rude thing to say to your client, I thought. "What about you, Darby?" I asked. "Are you ever going on a vacation?"

"I can't go on a vacation until I achieve my financial goals," she said, putting Twix on the leash.

She was the most focused twenty-three-year-old I had ever met. "What are your financial goals?"

"I am working on getting enough capital together to start my own business," she said as she walked out the door with the dog.

I thought about Darby as a business owner. She would probably be a great boss. She'd be telling everyone who looked stressed to take a vacation. I could go on vacation, but it would never be a real vacation because all my not-real jobs would follow me there. I could farm out assembling Clementine's lunch, maybe, and making toast for my family members, but those jobs were the easy ones, and it wasn't worth trying to vacation from them.

The door rattled but didn't open and then rattled again and didn't open, so finally I went over and opened it myself.

"Hola," said Betty, walking in with a poster board. She sat down at the kitchen table. Jack and Betty had the day off school.

"This is my chart about inequality," she announced, showing me the chart like the very good student she undoubtedly was. "It depicts how our economic bounty flows overwhelmingly to a small share of the population."

"Jack!" I yelled toward his tiny bedroom. "Betty's here!"

Betty's hair was still purple but styled differently, in swoops that flipped up in front and on the sides. It looked like a plane that wanted to take off. She was wearing the bag dress and the bag shoes again, or maybe her outfit was a different spin on the same bag design. There was probably a small signifier, I thought, that made it clear that this was a different iteration of trash bag dress from the one I had seen previously.

I knew this because although I might not be financially literate, I was fashion literate. I was self-taught in this literacy, as fashion wasn't anything I had studied growing up in Minnesota. The biggest sartorial revelation of my childhood was when I found out that goose-down-filled clothing existed. But I had enjoyed becoming fashion literate in college, when I'd started dating George. I enjoyed looking at clothes and learning about them and dressing up in interestingly constructed and colorful pieces. Clothing was a lot like architecture, like a puzzle demanding that you figure out how many shipping containers you could successfully fit on the rocky triangle of your body.

I am not sure how my fashion literacy serves me now, though. Maybe this knowledge would be useful if I had to pick out couture from the racks at the Salvation Army. If I ever had to discern crap fashion from couture to feed our family, I could, and then I would have a designer dress to put out alongside the cranky incense guy on Sixth Avenue, and I'd be part of the rummage sale there, out with the other vendors displaying their plastic place mats featuring times tables and outdated world maps. And my couture would sit there beside George's sixty-thousand-dollar not-an-ashtray, and we would be OK for a while longer, if it sold.

These are exactly the sort of thoughts, by the way, that *Think Your Way Rich* tells you to excise immediately, should you have them. You can't be thinking yourself rich when you are imagining yourself selling secondhand clothing next to the plastic place mat guy.

I am not sure how you are supposed to have a good wealth mindset, as the book called it, and also be conscious of wealth inequality. I am not talking about the mindset of a rich person where the wealth has already been made, and you just have it, and it's just sitting there in the backyard like a giant beehive, and you hire people to wear the protective suit and go out and check on it. Those people harvest the honey for you, and then come in and give it to you in a little jar that is perfect and sealed like a face cream, and you spread it on your toast, and as you chew the delectable honey toast, you decide which charity is worthy enough to receive your donations.

I am talking about the mindset of how you get that wealth in the first place, how you have to stoke your own honey hunger, and you have to be hungry as hell for honey because you have to step over the many other people who are also scrambling for honey in your quest to not become one of the many people to whom the honey is not going to disproportionately flow.

This is how the wealth mindset books help you, by banishing conflicting thoughts and feelings and keeping you focused on your goal. They help you put on the wealth mindset blinders so you can race to the wealth finish line, so you see only the *finish* and not, say, anyone else who is not getting money but may really need it.

I know this technique works because I have seen other people use it—other people like my father, for instance, and George. And OK, myself.

Second Winter

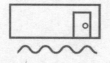

I BOUGHT CLEMENTINE A pair of rain boots online without asking her first. When she saw they were purple, she was aghast.

I repacked the boots in the box, printed out the return label and affixed it to the box, and then filled out the online form and submitted it. Immediately, I got an email back that said my return had been processed and the refund was back on my card.

That seemed weird, because the boots were still in my possession. They were sitting by the apartment door, waiting for our UPS man to come and take them. I realized the boots were an afterthought in this transaction.

It was so different from when I was a kid, before online shopping, when returning anything to the store required that you go to the store with the item and a story about what was wrong with it. You had to perform your return like you were on the high school debate team. Now it seemed like companies threw you a refund if you showed an *intent* to return the item.

It made me sad. The sixty-nine dollars I spent on my rain boots didn't seem important to the store anymore. This store was so huge that whatever I spent on my boots was play money. They could give me my sixty-nine dollars back a million times over and never miss it. But that sixty-nine dollars was still important to *me*.

I pushed that thought away and decided to book a hotel room for me and George. I booked it at my favorite hotel, the one hooked up to my credit card. It was a block from our apartment, on West Twenty-Eighth: the Boxy. I had sampled every brand of hotel in the company's portfolio at this point, and the Boxy wasn't the most luxurious, but I had found that "luxury," from the hotel group's perspective, only meant that the hotel lobby looked like a raccoon had poured gold and mirrors all over it.

The Boxy's schtick, aesthetically, was simple rather than shiny. The rooms were small for an American hotel, but they were well designed. If you wanted to sit in your hotel room, on a surface that wasn't your bed, you could avail yourself of the leather camp stool that was folded and hung on a peg on the wall. The bathroom had a shower with zero gold fixtures but excellent water pressure. The bathroom was separated from the bedroom by a pocket door. The room was neat, like a ship's cabin.

Going to the Boxy with George was exciting. We sauntered down the blocks between our apartment and the hotel like nothing was urgent at all. We held hands and then let them go and then held them again. We touched like doing so didn't have much value.

We were leaving the box of our apartment to go to another box that was our reward. We were rich in our many kinds of boxes. And the Boxy box was the most wonderful box of all because it was our secret box. No one knew we were there: not the kids, not the babysitter. We were in on something astonishing together, like two doves stashed in the tails of a magician's tux.

This particular time at the Boxy, we checked in and went up the elevator to the room that was only slightly different from the room we had had last time. We had gotten very adept at spotting the differences between similar rooms, to note a slightly better view, or a smidgen more square footage, or a more advantageous positioning of the bed. But most things in the room were the same, which was comforting. My enjoyment in sameness of hotel rooms was similar to Clementine's being soothed by a never-varying lunch.

We went into the room and took off our clothes unceremoniously. And then we got on the bed and just lay there together, me on top of him, a thin layer of electric warmth between us, like we were sitting in a lunch box, a sandwich made by god.

George and I never stayed at these hotels overnight. We came in, we screwed, we left. Usually George and I went to eat somewhere afterward, something simple. But this night, George said no, he wanted to go someplace cheaper than usual: a food court near Times Square.

My stomach sank when I heard him say that. Money.

I went where he wanted to go, though. It was nice for a food court, hidden on the second floor of a different hotel. We got fancy slices of pizza and ate them at a marble counter overlooking the street.

"Even when you think you're not spending money, you *are*," George reminded me.

I didn't want to talk about this on my date night. I thought about telling him my mantra—"Only poor people see obstacles"—but I didn't. Instead, I asked, "How is that even possible, George?"

"It takes money just to breathe in this town," he said with a sigh, looking down at the crowds headed to Broadway, each person's ticket costing hundreds of dollars.

I poked at a caramelized onion with my fork. That's how you knew the pizza was fancy: they gave you a fork.

"People created money, we should be able to destroy it," I said.

George chewed his slice. It was more expensive than a regular slice but less expensive than what we would have paid if we had eaten it in a real restaurant with waitstaff serving it to us on a tray.

"Do you know what would happen if people destroyed money? It would last like seven seconds. We'd just remake it again in a new form."

I regarded my triangle slice of pizza. It looked like our tick farm, if someone had taken a bite out of it.

"I mean, before there were dollars, there were Murano glass beads," he continued, waving his fork. "Now there's crypto."

2

DARBY WALKED INTO the apartment. I was sitting with my laptop open, googling rainfall showerheads.

"What's that you're wearing?" I asked.

"Oh, it's something I made for my accessories class," she said. "I'm field-testing it."

"It's . . . a leash?"

"Well, the design is based off a bondage harness design, so, yes," she said, fingering the strap that ran across her chest. "But this is full-grain Italian leather. It's meant to be worn outside your clothes, as an embellishment." She picked up Twix.

I sat there trying to think of something nice to say about it.

"I've been meaning to tell you," she continued. "Twix told me on our walk that the dog food you're buying is more expensive than it needs to be."

I looked at her and blinked.

"Just thought you'd want to know. Maybe you could save a little money." She winked at me as she departed with the dog.

Maybe I should rethink the fact that Darby has a key to our apartment, I thought. I had already cut her services to two mornings a week. Our new arrangement was outside the Canine Companions contract, which was something neither I nor Darby was supposed to do, but Darby OK'd the terms when I proposed them. She charged me less, since she didn't have to give the service a cut. She also didn't send me any more number-filled emails. She just walked the dog during her off-hours on the days we agreed on, and I paid her cash once a month.

I walked the dog more myself, then, and that's how I noticed that Twix seemed upset. Outside, she was barking more when I walked her. Inside, she was chewing George's dirty socks and leaving them around the house in little balls. I had thought dogs were supposed to act ashamed when they did something like that, but that wasn't Twix's style. She led me to the socks and then sat there looking at me expectantly, like I was going to understand what she was trying to communicate.

I couldn't figure out why she would be upset. I thought I gave her everything you were supposed to give a dog: treats, walks, a rain-coat, boots, a Halloween costume, and a microchip. I let her sleep on my head. I guess I could have tried training her to do tricks, but I thought the kindest thing I could do, as a dog owner, was let her be a regular dog, or as regular as a dog can be while wearing an argyle sweater.

This philosophy extended to my children as well. I tried to let my children be regular children as much as I could, but it was hard to know what a "regular" child was. I had lived a long time, and met many odd people, and was a weirdo myself, but children in general were still among the most wonderfully strange creatures I had ever met. Our dog was a factory-manufactured cookie in comparison.

In walking the dog more, I discovered something new about her, too, which was that she came with a built-in accessory that was not advertised in the puppy store: a chicken bone radar. Twix could smell a chicken bone under a UPS truck half a block away. Before I got a dog, I had not known this fact: there is chicken fricking everywhere in New York City. Not live chickens, not the real, living animals that naturally aerate the earth when they walk around, scratching its surface. The chicken in New York City is roasted, barbecued, nugget-ified, ground, and put on sticks. You can't go twenty feet in this town without stumbling on some chicken. There is chicken in every restaurant, deli, and food truck. The mayor is eating chicken at Gracie Mansion. The prisoners in Rikers are eating chicken. The schoolchildren in the lunchrooms are eating chicken. There is chicken on the pizza at the slice place. The sky in New York City is falling with chicken. People are walking down the street gnawing on chicken legs like Henry VIII.

And I know this because every time I walk the dog, I have to make sure that she doesn't eat chicken bones, because people on West Twenty-Seventh Street are apparently shopping at Irritable Bowel Syndrome and taking improv comedy classes while simultaneously shoving chicken legs in their mouths and throwing the bones in the street.

And once a day when my dog poops out her dainty little poop, a poop that is formed from dog food that has chicken in it—because how could it not have chicken in it?—I pick it up carefully with a plastic bag and throw it in the trash, as if dogs and their small creations are what is so toxic in this town.

3

I WENT TO VISIT Walter at his studio in Long Island City. He had recently begun a new series of paintings featuring stacks of cash.

I saw one of the new canvases as soon as I walked in. It was an eight-by-ten-foot painting of a woman's well-manicured hand holding a stack of fanned-out hundred-dollar bills.

"Whoa!" I exclaimed.

"I was going to call it *Stripper Cash*," Walter said, getting up from the easel where he was sitting in front of a cheeseburger painting. "But maybe it should be something more highbrow."

I sat down on a metal chair near his easel. "*Tuition?*"

"Ha-ha," he said, not laughing.

Walter sat across a coffee table from me on a metal stool. There was a bowl of hard candies on the table. I took a red one, unwrapped it, and popped it in my mouth. It was the familiar, unreal cherry. Clementine's favorite.

"So how's your wrongdoing going?" Walter asked. He was fingering a pen. He always had some kind of mark-making tool in his hands.

"Not great," I admitted.

"You're still taking care of the kids?" Walter had a daughter, but she was grown, married, and had just had twins.

"I haven't abandoned them on the side of the road, if that's what you mean."

"That's good. A lot of people wait until the kids are gone to have their nervous breakdowns."

"You haven't," I said.

"I have to work." He set the pen down and began cleaning a brush.

"But I thought visual artists were supposed to be the most debauched of all the creatives!"

"I don't know about that," he said, petting the brush. "They *are* the poorest, though."

"Everyone's poor," I said, reaching for another red candy.

He looked at me skeptically over the top of his glasses. "You're not poor," he said.

"I'm not rich enough to buy *Stripper Cash*," I retorted. "How much will your dealer get for that? Six figures?"

"Hope so." He smiled.

"Why do art journalists always say that paintings 'fetch' prices, like paintings are dogs running after money?"

"It's an Englishism," Walter replied. "You can look it up in the *OED*."

I wondered what it would be like to put a painting up for auction like it was a dog trained to chase after cash. If I had a dog like that, rather than one who chewed socks, I wouldn't be sweating a garbage beach house, that's for sure.

I sat back and looked at the money painting. "What should I do? I just feel so helpless all the time," I said plaintively.

"Everyone feels helpless," he said. He turned to pluck a green candy out of the bowl. "That's why there's art."

4

A T 6:00 THE next morning, Twix woke me up by licking my face. I reluctantly pulled on my sweatpants, slid on my jacket and mules, and took her outside.

I pulled her away from the empty pizza box on the sidewalk in front of our building. It was a pain to take her outside, but I was happy she was basically housebroken. That was all I ever expected her to learn. It was a relief to feel like her education was complete. She knew how to pee and poop outside; she had her puppy PhD. Anything else she wanted to learn in this life was, as Chase referred to it, "enrichment." My own children's early childhood would have been so much more manageable if I had only been responsible for getting them to make their numbers in the right place and not for this other thing I slowly realized I had to do, which was stoke wonder in them every second.

I tried to lead Twix toward the spindly tree in front of our building, but she sat firmly in the center of the sidewalk, resisting my tug. Suddenly, she peed there while looking directly at me.

"What's wrong, girl?" I asked. I had become one of those women who talks to their dog.

"Do you know where some families live?" she asked me.

I had imagined what my dog had been saying to me for so long it didn't seem that surprising when she actually spoke. I had a second where I wondered if I was having a cognitive distortion, but then I decided no, animals have been talking since the days of Aesop, and that was the sixth century BC.

"Do I know where some families live . . ." I said slowly. "Um, in beach houses?"

"On mountains of garbage!" she spat. "And do you know what those families eat on those mountains of garbage?"

I felt a twinge of sadness that "beach houses" had been wrong. "Do I know what those families eat on those mountains of garbage . . ." I repeated. "Dog cookies?"

Twix looked at me, incredulous. "They eat garbage!"

This wasn't the conversation I dreamed I would one day have with my dog. The conversation I dreamed I would one day have with my dog was that she would tell me what a great dog owner I was.

"So what are you going to do about your participation in this system?" Twix prodded.

"What system?" I asked.

"The system that confers no value on your work?!"

"Oh, that system," I said.

"Why don't you start a revolution demanding that men do more domestic work and child-rearing?" she asked, walking a few paces to sniff something on the sidewalk.

Snowy wouldn't talk like this to Tintin, I thought. "George does a lot of work around the house," I said meekly.

"Not as much as he could," she snapped. "Not if it were fifty-fifty."

"But he supports us," I said.

"But you also work," Twix said.

"Yes, but my work doesn't make us any money," I said. I actually felt like I was getting onto solid ground here. This wasn't any more wacky than any interspecies conversations in Aesop's work, like the one where a frog talks to boys about death. My dog and I were having a serious conversation. We were talking about money. I talked about money—to myself, at least—all the time. It was something I knew something about. What would I have done if Twix asked me about the beauty of sea anemones?

"Aren't you going to do something about this unfair structure you're stuck in?" she snapped. "Aren't you going to demand money for your work?"

"Well, I get paid, in a way," I said defensively. "I am provided for by George. And I am getting a beach house."

"Yes, but that's not money for *your* work," she retorted. "Don't you wish you got money for the good work you do? Piles and piles of it?"

She arched her back to poop. It was refreshing to see such lack of shame. Why was shame so intrinsic to the human experience? I tried to think of something good about shame. I came up with one: it enabled the miracle that was a Japanese toilet that played music to cover your gassy sounds.

I picked up Twix's poop with the bag. It was warm.

"Yes, I wish I had piles of money for my work," I admitted, holding the bag by my fingertips and carrying it to the corner trash can.

"Well, you could get a lot of people together and create a revolution around pay for care work," she said, as we began to walk back to the building.

"You have an awful lot of opinions about money for someone who gets universal basic income and cradle-to-grave health care," I retorted.

5

BEA WROTE TO tell me that the date for the Home Aesthetics Committee meeting had been set. It would be in four weeks.

I was elated we finally had a date. I told Marianne about it. She suggested a time for me and George to meet at her office to talk about it beforehand. I pulled my dress sweatpants out of the bottom of my drawer, and George and I went over there.

Marianne's office was a little more cluttered than the last time. The conference table was covered with piles of papers and samples of wood, tile, and marble. The blocks from my previous visit had been put away. No more playing around, I guessed.

Marianne looked totally put together, as usual. She had on a slim-fitting dress in a yellow-and-black geometric print. She had lined her eyes in black eyeliner and covered the lids in a pinky gold shadow, which looked all the more striking with her shaved head. She made room for us to sit down.

She assured us that she had been through these types of meetings before. They were just a formality. All these people wanted to do was get a general idea of "who you were and what you were doing," which seemed like a lot for anyone besides the IRS to know about us.

We should really start putting the house together *now*, Marianne advised. Don't wait for the committee's approval, which was going to happen. And all the construction would take place off-site, so it wasn't like our beginning now was going to disturb our Crashing Sound neighbors. If we did it that way, starting to build now, then after the meeting, the house would be ready to go. We wouldn't have wasted all this time. We would come out with the approval of the housing association, and then the house would be ready to get on the flatbed truck and start its journey from Vermont to its forever home.

"What if it's not approved?" George asked.

"It will be approved," Marianne said, picking up her chunky, black-framed glasses from the conference table and waving them dismissively. "I've been through a lot of these. They're routine! And meanwhile we can buy the shipping containers. It takes a while for them to get here, and I want to make sure we get really good ones."

"Well, if we get the containers, we have to build the house," George countered. "There will be no backing out after we become the proud owners of four used shipping containers."

"Not necessarily," Marianne said. "If you had to, you could always resell them."

I saw George's face light up. I knew what he was thinking: he could flip them.

"Can we get them at a discount?" George asked.

Marianne chuckled. "They're already being sold to us at a discount. But I'll look into getting a bigger discount. It depends on what they've had in them and how many trips they've taken."

"How vintage they are," George said, smiling.

"Exactly," Marianne replied.

"We get everything on sale," I said apologetically. "Even our dog."

There were lots of details still to cover, but because of all the budget cuts, the details weren't that exciting to me. They weren't like the small details on a piece of couture, the signifiers that were going to reward the sharp observer. All our choices were more like, do you want the white inexpensive kitchen cupboards or the off-white inexpensive kitchen cupboards? I was just glad Marianne was keeping track of it all.

"Do we need to talk about the budget again?" Marianne asked, looking at me.

"No," I said quickly.

"Let's go over it briefly," Marianne said, gazing at George. "So we cut out the garage. . . ."

"We cut out the garage?!" George asked in disbelief, looking at me.

"Just for now," I said, patting his hand.

"I think we need to lose the basement as well," Marianne said.

"Lose the basement? But what about storage?!" George cried.

"It's the basement or the pool. Do you need a pool?" Marianne said.

I shuddered. "We need a pool," I declared.

"We also need a basement," George affirmed.

"I think there is a way to include a small basement and still stay on your budget," Marianne said diplomatically, looking down at the plans.

George looked relieved. We talked about details for a while longer. Then George took a deep breath and peered at me skeptically. "We're probably not going to get this house built anyway," he said. "So it doesn't matter what it says on this piece of paper—none of it's real."

He pushed his chair back from the conference table, indicating that he was ready to go.

I got up, too. "Should we do anything else to prepare for the meeting?" I asked. The words had flown out of my mouth before I could stop them. I had to get out of this habit of always trying to add more work to my jobs.

Marianne put her glasses on. Architects love their funky glasses, I've noticed. Stylish glasses are like little billboards they wear to advertise how creatively they see the world. "You don't have to do anything," she said, looking at me via her billboard. "I'll do all the talking."

I smiled wanly.

"Just remember," she said, raising her index finger, "architecture is about storytelling."

6

WHEN I GOT my first job, as a fourteen-year-old, I was supposed be sixteen. I lied about my age. At the time I thought this little maneuver was really edgy, but now I am sure my boss knew and didn't care.

I needed my parents to drive me to work—to Sammy's Italian Ristorante—so I told them about my job after I got it. They were proud of my gumption but perplexed as to why I wanted to get a dishwashing job on top of my already busy schedule with school and homework.

I don't know that I could have explained it. When I saw the HELP WANTED sign in the mall, it hit me like a lightning bolt: Dishwashing is something I can do. For *money*.

Of course, our plastic dishpan looked very tame indeed when I stood on the rubber mat at Sammy's, in front of an industrial sink so large I could have bathed in it. The sprayer hung down on a spring from the ceiling, bouncing around me like a giant cobra. When I caught it by the neck and pressed the lever, it emitted a scalding hiss of water.

I stood there for eight hours at a time, rinsing dishes in a cloud of steam before putting them in the giant dishwasher. That combination of substances—marinara, steam, dish soap—has a very particular smell that I will be nauseated by for the rest of my life.

What got me through my brief stint of this work was, naturally, the relationships. I made friends with the waiters, who were only a couple of years older than me. One of them, an olive-skinned kid named Angelo, went into the walk-in cooler with me to illicitly snack on spoonfuls of cookie dough from an industrial-size tub. In some ways, this was a rehearsal for the secret box of my hotel room. The walk-in cooler in Minneapolis was my very first illicit box with a boy in it.

I was paid my first real money—my own money!—on this job. I cashed my checks and kept my cash in a metal lockbox on my dresser that I unlocked with a tiny silver key. Occasionally I would open the box and count my money. I was proud of this money but discouraged by its paucity. I had worked so many hours, standing in a stinky, tropical cloud, inhaling hot, wet food fumes while my hands turned raw. It seemed like I should have been paid a zillion dollars for that. This was my first inkling that money was not going to come easy for me.

And yet there was incalculable satisfaction in the fact that the dishwasher, which had been off-limits to me for so long, which had sat in my own house and mocked me with its parched maw of cookies, was now under my command. There was a sweet vindication that the first time I got to use a dishwasher for its intended purpose, I was paid for it.

7

GEORGE GOT THE Placatrex gig! We were really excited.

"Maybe this could be the start of my being the go-to guy for drugs," he said, sipping coffee as he got ready to go to the studio to record.

"I don't think you mean that the way it sounds," I said, looking askance at Clementine, who was getting ready for school.

"You know what I mean," he said, beginning his warm-up: "HA! HA! HA!"

"What's Placatrex, exactly?" I asked.

"I'll find out today," he said.

Later that morning, after I walked the dog, my device buzzed. It was Marianne, calling to say that she thought she had found some good shipping containers for us.

"They're in great shape, no dings, but their cargo is a little odd," she said. "I wanted to run it by you."

"Is that what you meant when you said you wanted us to get good shipping containers?" I asked. "Good cargo?"

"Well, that's part of it," she said.

"So what are they filled with . . . Legos?" I asked. I had read about some Lego-filled containers that had fallen off a ship off the coast of England, causing Legos to wash up on a nearby beach for months. Parents took their kids there to collect Legos like they were seashells. It sounded cool in a postapocalyptic way.

"No," she said. "Cat food."

I grimaced.

"Well, it's *gourmet* cat food," she said.

"Marianne," I said. "We are dog people."

"That's what I thought," she said. "I'll keep looking."

It was midmorning. I did laundry, put away dishes, sent emails, paid bills, ate lunch, bought stuff, walked Twix, picked up Clementine from the bus stop, and all of a sudden it was 4:00 p.m. Betty and Jack were at the kitchen table. Betty's hair was pink now. She was still wearing the trash bag ensemble.

"You have several versions of that outfit?" I asked her.

"This is my uniform," she said.

I raised an eyebrow at her.

"Lots of famous people have uniforms," she explained. "They have several copies of the same outfit so they don't have to expend any mental energy thinking about what to put on in the morning. It helps free them up for thinking about more important things." She emphasized "more important things" and then looked at me meaningfully, as if to imply that whatever she was thinking about was more important than whatever I was thinking about.

"I have a uniform, too," I said. "Black sweatpants."

"*This* outfit actually helps the environment," she replied. "It's a dress shaped like a trash bag to call attention to our unsustainable waste disposal practices. Plus, a percentage of the money I paid for the dress is used to fund select clean-water nonprofits."

I radiate love, I thought to myself, as I left her and Jack in the kitchen and went into the bathroom to fly some cream into my face.

GEORGE CAME HOME from the Placatrex gig that evening and plopped down beside me on the couch. Something had gone wrong.

"Everything started out OK," he reported despondently. "I had done my warm-ups, I was in the booth, I recorded the script. But then I had to do the legalese."

"The what?"

"The side effects. They're required now. And it's a completely different type of reading!"

"What did you have to say?"

"All the crap that can go wrong when you take Placatrex! The line was—listen to this—'Side effects of Placatrex are uncommon and include hemorrhoids, hypnagogic hallucinations, and vascular ischemia caused by thrombosis.'"

"Whoa," I said, impressed.

"And every time that I managed to say it without tripping up, the copywriter would say, 'OK, great, now can you speed it up?'!"

"Oh geez," I sympathized.

"I swear, they're not going to use it, though. I can feel it! They sent me home with big fake smiles!"

"You have a beautiful voice, George," I said reassuringly. "Something else will come up."

"No, I'm doomed! The only things that regular guys like me can sell anymore are drugs and sandwiches. If I can't voice those, I'm screwed! I'll never get to cars!"

I was going to continue reassuring him, but just then Twix came into the room. I looked at her like, don't you dare use your voice right now. And she didn't.

9

I WENT TO THE puppy store to get some treats for Twix. I was wandering around when I saw a spray that was supposed to take all the pee and poop smell out of the carpet after your dog had an accident. "Nature's Miracle," it was called.

I am intrigued by nature. "What's *in* this?" I asked the guy who was restocking the shelves.

"A miracle," he said with a wink, and I didn't get any more out of him.

I wasn't squeamish about cleaning up dog pee or poop if it occasionally appeared on our floor because I had already been through toilet training my kids. Here is a little secret: dealing with dog poop is much easier than dealing with kid poop. I don't know why more people don't acknowledge this. I think it's because humans need a poop villain, and the villain we have found is dogs. We need to use dogs for this role because otherwise we would see who the real villains are: babies. And no one wants to believe that villain babies exist, particularly villain-baby parents.

If you look it at objectively, though, you can see where the poop problem is in our society, and it isn't with dogs. There is an entire social and legal structure built around the collection and disposal of dog poop, and everyone knows how it works. In New York City, at least, if I am going to walk my dog, I just go out there, in the street, with my dog and a plastic bag. The bag is generally a camouflage-green color that does the opposite of what camouflage is supposed to do. It telegraphs its existence far and wide. This camouflage bag is much bigger than I am ever going to need for my dog's poop, but the point is not that it covers the poop. The point is that it covers my hand, because the bag functions as a poop bag *and* a poop mitten. Why it's designed without a thumb, I don't know. But these poop mittens, as crappy as they are, are genius compared to the tools on offer for changing a baby's diaper. And that's too bad, because when I was in the years of changing my kids' diapers, I could have used a poop mitten. For my soul.

The stuff that came out of my cherubic children's rears was routinely, um, satanic. And all that modern society had to offer me for that task was wipes. Wipes! Just the name lets you know that there isn't going to be any containing of anything there. With wipes, you're just cleaning your kid's bottom like you're not even dealing with poop at all. You're just shining your kid's rear windshield.

Here is what I would routinely do and think nothing of it: I would be in the car, on a little trip, and I would smell something infernal and realize that I had to stop and change the baby's diaper. I would have to do this immediately so the baby did not get a rash, because although I could deny many other qualities about baby poop, I could not deny that its skin-corroding effects are on par with hydrochloric acid.

So I would pull the rental car over to the side of the road and lay my baby down in the wayback. And then I would use the wipes to shine her rear windshield, piling the dirty wipes in the soiled diaper.

Just the piling of poopy wipes in a poopy diaper would be enough of a task, you would think. But in a moment of insane ambition—really a megalomania more suited to an architect, I see now—I then engaged in the common diapering tactic of trying to use the little pieces of diaper tape, which were no longer sticky because my kid had worn the diaper for hours, to fold the whole diaper-wipe-poop pile into a closed container.

I repeat: I would stand on the side of the highway, with tractor-trailers thundering by me, holding a half-naked, crying child, as I tried to transform a poopy diaper, poopy wipes, and poop itself into what was essentially an origami box.

It's as if parents can't acknowledge how insane this whole situation is, because if they did, there would be a societal breakdown. Parents can't look this situation in the eye because they have to change diapers for *so long*. I more or less completely house-trained my discount dog in two months. My gifted and talented children? Two *years*. By the time I was on to our second kid, I was so deep in my diapering denial that she could have shat out a nuclear warhead, and I would have just stood there like, damn, how am I gonna fit *this* in the Diaper Genie?

This is why we get a viral video when a parent changes his kid's diaper in the airplane seat next to a nonparent. Because nonparents are not in the type of denial that parents have to be in in order to survive the diapering years. Parents have to be blind like this, because baby poop can be unspeakable. My dog that we rescued from the puppy store window has always had predictable, nicely formed, poop-like poops. My healthy kid, born in a hospital, scoring 10 on the Apgar, spent one memorable luxury vacation shitting worms.

10

ARE WE PART of the one percent?" Twix asked me as we were walking on our block one morning.

"Definitely not," I replied.

"Ten percent?"

"No."

"Twenty percent?"

"Umm . . . maybe?"

"Then let's give away, like, fifty percent of our money."

I glared at her. "Where are you getting this math?"

"I'm making it up," she said, sniffing a flattened brown bag on the street that revealed itself, upon closer inspection, to be a run-over rat.

"What about the children?!" I asked her, dragging her away from the rat corpse.

"Yes, the chicken need to be considered. There should be more chicken rights."

"No, the *children*."

"Oh! Kids can make do with so little," she said conspiratorially.

She stopped to do #1. "You know, you should also really try to love bigger than you do," she continued. "You should love everyone you meet."

I was fuming that my dog was lecturing me like this. "Have you ever actually tried that?" I griped. "Do you know what kind of internal energy it takes to let all your walls down and experience the world like that?"

"Yes, I do," she said sassily, wiggling as she walked. "Because dogs do that all the time."

11

GEORGE AND I went to Marianne's office because she wanted to speak in person about what she called "next steps." Now that we had the house down on paper, we needed to talk to the contractors in Vermont who would be tricking out the containers. She had set up a call with them.

When we walked into her office, I saw that her conference table had accumulated even more papers and samples. Marianne was dressed impeccably in a black blouse that jutted out from the sides like it had armature underneath it. Her glasses had a red stripe running along the top and looked Italian and costly. She wore them on top of her head.

As we sat down, she told us the workers' names: Vinnie and Frank. She leaned in. "They're furries," she added, smiling.

George laughed.

"What's a furry?" I asked.

"They're like the ComicCon people," George explained. We had been to several ComicCons with Jack and Clementine. The attendees who dressed up in character were my favorite part.

"I think you'll like them," Marianne added, fussing with the computer.

"How did you get connected with contractor furries?" I asked Marianne.

Marianne pulled her glasses down over her eyes to look at me. "I met them through another container job," she said. "They're *very* inexpensive."

I didn't argue with that.

The screen pinged. Marianne adjusted the brightness as the image came to life. "Hi, you two!" she exclaimed, grinning.

Vinnie and Frank appeared. They were fresh-faced white guys. I was surprised by how young they looked—they seemed only a little older than Jack. Vinnie was dark-haired and chubby and had acne, while Frank was skinny with a sweet face and blond hair that stuck straight up. I wondered what kinds of animals they were, in their furry lives. I could picture them both as woodland creatures: a fox and a rabbit.

"Let's talk about beach houses!" Marianne yelled, like a game show host.

Vinnie and Frank seemed easygoing and excited about the project. They explained how the four containers would be stacked, two on top of two. Windows would be installed on the two far ends of this container-made box, Frank explained. You couldn't put much of any windows on the sides, he said, because if you did, the structure would collapse on itself like a bubble.

After going over some more details, we said goodbye to them. I was feeling pretty good about it all as Marianne spread her renderings out on the table. I took a closer look.

"Wait, aren't we missing some elements here?" I asked, alarmed.

Marianne spread her palms over the drawings and looked at me. "I cut two of the bedrooms and two of the baths because it just wasn't feasible given the container configuration and your budget," she said coolly.

My jaw dropped. "When were you going to tell us that?!"

"I'm telling you now," she said, pushing her glasses higher on her nose. "And the granite kitchen counter you chose is prohibitively expensive," she added, passing me another paper with the estimates. "So that had to go, too."

Marianne was erasing all the stuff on my vision board! What kind of trick was it, that she was vanishing my house rather than varnishing it? Why were some people allowed to manifest the things on their vision boards and other people were allowed to erase them? It wasn't even like I was asking to manifest all that much! I just wanted to take a piece of leftover junk and live in it! I was like a raccoon—wait, not even a raccoon. A mouse! I was making a mouse house out of garbage! How pathetic was it that I even had to get a vision board to manifest that in the first place?!

"So here is what we have now," Marianne said, looking at her list. "You'll have two bedrooms. The primary bedroom will be upstairs, and you will have your own bathroom there."

I imagined my toilet. That calmed me down.

"Downstairs, you'll have the second bedroom—the kids will have to share, or I can put in a wall and make the kids two micro bedrooms—and another bathroom."

"Micro bedrooms?" I asked.

"It's a new term," she said. "They're private rooms—just, ah, compact."

I liked that there was a fancy new name for what we had made in our city apartment with our temporary wall.

"Plus, you'll have kitchen and living space," she continued. "And then you'll also have the gravel driveway and a pool."

"A heated pool?" I pleaded.

"Unheated," she declared.

"It looks so small," I whined, forgetting that I had once been enthralled with the idea of a port-a-potty next to a yurt.

I could see George panicking. There would be no place for him to store his treasures.

Marianne understood. "Listen, it's a beach house," she said to us in a tone you would use if you were advertising a drug to calm your stomach issues. "You use it in the summer. You're outside all day long. Two beds—three, if two of them are micro-size—and two baths for a family of four is more than you need!"

"But the garage sales and thrift stores are so great out there! Where will I put all my finds?" George sounded wistful.

"You do have the small basement," Marianne reminded him. "But you have to stay focused on more important things. Do you want a house or not?"

I waited to hear George say, "No."

But he didn't. He didn't say anything at all, in fact, as Vinnie and Frank smiled and nodded at us encouragingly, like parents do at children who are failing at something, but the parents want the children to keep trying.

12

THE NEXT DAY, I was in the apartment on West Twenty-Seventh Street, sitting in our bedroom with the door closed. I had a session with Alice. I wanted to cancel it, but I knew if I canceled she was going to charge me anyway. So I went.

I was really upset about all the things I wasn't getting in my rapidly diminishing beach house, but I didn't want to talk to her about that. If we were going to talk about money, I only wanted to talk about money in general. I wanted to talk about money in the abstract. Money as a concept. Not *my* money.

I took a bite of a Generosity bar as I started off by declaring that financial literacy was a crock. It's mostly good for rich people, I said, because it helps them believe that poor people are only poor because they can't read money. "Financial literacy makes it sound like poor people just need a little help with their money decoding skills," I griped. "But the problem is more likely that they have been the victims of years of calculated, systemic disempowerment."

"Interesting," she said. Alice was sitting in her office in the city. The rock around her neck was smaller than usual. It could have been any of the ones I had found in the creek with my mother.

"It's similar to the kind of wordplay that is happening with 'food insecurity,'" I continued, on a roll now that we weren't talking about anything relating to me. "'Food insecurity' puts the onus of the problem in the wrong place. Food is not insecure. People are starving."

"Yes, but you can't deny that skills with money are things people can learn—how to use a checkbook, how to balance it, or the benefits of budgeting and saving," Alice pointed out. "And it's good for people, especially those without much money, to learn about the scams and pitfalls they can be victimized by."

Alice chewed on the end of her pen. She was taking notes. It always felt flattering to me that I was a subject worth taking notes on, like I was deep and complex, like a great work of literature.

"Sure," I said. "But what about all the scams that are just built into the system? Like the eight billion dollars that the top four banks make annually off overdraft fees?"

Alice blinked at me. I was proud of myself for spouting that factoid. Betty had told it to me.

"And besides," I continued, "isn't behavior with money most similar to behavior with food? You learn it first from your family, and if there is dysfunction, it gets passed down like any other screwy family behavior?"

"That can be true," she allowed.

"People who grow up with more money frequently learn different behaviors than people who grow up with less money," I continued, not mentioning that I did not balance my checkbook. "But you can't assume that people with more money always pass down healthier behaviors. What they do pass down, often, is wealth. Which is protective."

"Well, you didn't grow up poor," she said, clearly wanting to put the focus back on me. "Let's go over your mantras again."

Therapy could be so annoying, I thought. I took a sip of water. Those Generosity bars go down like wet concrete.

I closed my eyes. "All is well," I intoned. "I radiate love."

I opened my eyes.

"Great. You're doing great," Alice said.

"How can you say that?" I carped. I was thinking about my shrinking beach house.

Her eyes narrowed. "You're doing great," she said evenly. "Because you're not throwing water bottles at people's heads."

Now I was angry. "Well, maybe I should be throwing *more* water bottles! Maybe when I was throwing water bottles, I was actually more in tune with what was happening in the world! Maybe *then* I was fully alive!"

We sat in silence for a few seconds.

"Did you ever go hungry when you were a child?" Alice asked me gently, fingering her rock.

I wasn't about to go there. "Alice, you know there was always a box of cookies in our dishwasher," I snapped.

13

MARIANNE CALLED WITH a lead on some new containers. "They're in Malaysia now. Like new!"

"What's in them?" I asked.

"Frozen chicken nuggets," she said.

I was disappointed. Why had I imagined that shipping containers were only full of cool stuff like Legos, sports cars, and stolen art?

"Marianne, our son, Jack, is a vegetarian," I said. "I don't think that nuggets are a good choice for us."

"But they're frozen! And they're in fun shapes, like dinosaurs!"

"Marianne," I began.

"Listen, you don't have to tell your son about your shipping container backstory—I'm only telling *you* as a client courtesy!"

"I just don't think so," I said, holding firm.

"Come *on*! I can't keep chasing these backstories down!" she griped. "The container world is in a terrible mess, did you know that? More containers have fallen off ships in the past four months than are typically lost in a year!"

I flashed on an image of an ocean filled with container ships, viewed from overhead, as if illustrated by Richard Scarry. Ships were being driven by hapless rabbits and dogs, and they were all crashing into each other, with the containers falling overboard.

"I understand," I said, "but I don't think it's too much to ask to get used shipping containers—in which I am going to be *living*—that have had a good life! And if they can't have had a *good* life, then at least I want them to have had a *neutral* life."

"What's a neutral life?!" she asked.

I thought about it. "One without any death in it?"

She snorted. "Everything contains death, Shelly! That's how life is!"

"I realize that! But I just don't want any death in the backstory of our house!"

"Well, I hate to tell you what actually happens in shipping containers these days," she sniped. "Desperate people die in them."

"I *know* that, Marianne."

"You're awfully fussy for someone who is building on such a tight budget," she said.

"I'm not fussy," I said haughtily, in a move I had learned from the moms at Chase. "I'm discerning."

Marianne snorted.

"Just try one more time for us, Marianne," I implored. "Please."

14

A WEEK LATER, GEORGE and I were in the apartment having breakfast. I was unwrapping my egg sandwich from the corner deli.

"Don't throw that foil away!" George cried. "We can reuse it!"

I closed my eyes and exhaled as I folded the tinfoil into a neat square. "Have you thought about a name for the beach house?" I asked him.

George looked up from his device for a second. "Bleak House!"

I smirked as I poured myself some coffee and sat on the couch. Some people at the beach did name their houses, and sometimes the names were really fancy. Like, someone at the beach really has a house named Coxwould.

I guess that shouldn't be surprising, though. The Hamptons, after all, is an area known for its wealthy debauchery. The Hamptons didn't start out debauched, though. It started out as plain old land, period. It sat there and was made by god or not, depending on your thinking on god, and it had all the attendant nature—i.e., screwing and carnage—going on in it.

I researched it one day online as I was looking for a good head massager. The Springs was originally inhabited by the Montauk tribe. Starting around 1875, the tribe rented out parcels of land for pasturage through a company that paid the tribe an annuity. But the shareholders of the company disagreed over how to handle the land. After a court fight, the lands were sold at public auction, and the proceeds were distributed equally among the white people who lived there—but not among the members of the tribe.

A developer named Arthur Benson then purchased almost ten thousand acres from the East Hampton Trustees, although the land was still arguably owned by the Montauk. Benson sold five thousand acres of that to the Long Island Railroad and removed the Montauk still living in the area to inexpensive plots nearby. This move was not voluntary. According to John A. Strong, president of the Suffolk County Archaeological Association, "The houses at Montauk were either moved to Freetown or were burned to make sure that the people did not return."

In 1906, the Montauk people sued to expel Benson and the developers from their lands. But Benson and his colleagues hired expensive lawyers, and after many court battles, in October 1910, a judge ruled that the Montauk had in fact sold their land, and further, were no longer a tribe. The Montauk appealed again and again, but the court's decision was upheld.

The Montauk have never stopped fighting that erasure. In 2013, the New York State Assembly voted to approve the Montaukett Act, which would have reversed the state supreme court decision that declared the Montauk tribe extinct. The bill was vetoed by Governor Andrew Cuomo in 2013 and again in 2017. Reacting to the veto in 2017, Chief Robert Pharaoh told the *East Hampton Star*: "All you've got to do is turn on the news. This world is not for the poor. It's all just a game."

George looked up from his device. "Let's name the place Tick Farm," he said.

"But that was our name for the land," I protested. "Now we have a house on the land. You name the house, not the land."

"What about farms?" he protested. "When you name a farm, you're naming the land, the house, the barn, the stables, the pond, the horses, the cows, all of it."

"Yes, but we don't have a farm. We're not farming the ticks. The ticks are just there, multiplying, because that's what ticks do."

I saw his eyes light up. "I wonder if there's some way we can harvest our ticks and sell them. We could be like that lady who sells Hamptons Sea Salt in fancy glass bottles."

George really was a natural salesman. "Interesting," I said.

15

I SIGNED JACK AND me up for a one-day glassblowing experience
at a place in Brooklyn, but I didn't want to tell George about it
because it was really pricey. I considered telling him that I was going
to make some Murano glass beads for when our monetary system
collapsed but then I decided to just enjoy the time doing something
different with my son without thinking about the cost of it.

It seems like this is a lot of what parenting is these days, if you
have the money: you pay people to help you and your kid interact
with the world without hurting yourselves. Although you may hurt
yourself anyway, and that's why you sign the waiver. It's not like
when I was a kid and you just opened the door and went outside
without paying for it and without signing anything beforehand, and
there was no lawyer-god watching over you when you interacted
with the world, for the times when you and the world got into a
tussle and you lost.

There was a lawyer-god watching over us at the glassblowing
place, though, and I know because I signed the twelve-page waiver
beforehand. I thought of that waiver when Jack and I used the big

metal stick—the punty—to get a glob of molten glass from the insanely hot glass furnace, and then we poked at it with the instructor's help before reheating it in what is called the "glory hole."

Jack is nothing if not versed in pirate lore. He knows what a glory hole is, and when the instructor said the words, he made a face like "cringe."

Jack was working on making a small footed bowl. In order to make the bowl part of the bowl, you actually had to blow a bubble in the glass. That's what the bowl was—a bubble that had collapsed on itself, like the housing market bubble some finance writers say we are experiencing now.

Jack knelt down and blew the molten glass through the long tube. As he did this, I helped him by twirling the tube so that molten glass would remain on the end of the tube and not be pulled by gravity to the floor.

After Jack blew the bubble and it had collapsed and hardened into a bowl shape, he tapped the bowl off the tube and stuck the bowl on a molten base and then carried the bowl and base in metal tongs to sit in an area to cool. He was excited about what he had made. It wasn't symmetrical or perfect, but there was no doubt it was a bowl and could hold things. It came into the world like the rest of us, soft and hot and wet, and now it was cooling and drying, and we would know it was finished when it could be held and broken.

16

I'VE FOUND YOUR containers," Marianne announced over the phone. "They're in Shanghai."

I was looking at my vision board. It had almost nothing on it now that Marianne had stripped so many things from our house. There was only my picture of my Toto toilet and images of different colors of gravel.

"What's in them?"

"Shelves!" she announced brightly.

"Shelves?" I was disappointed.

"Yes, shelves. The ship will dock in Boston and then the shelves will get picked up by an office supply store."

Shelves were not interesting things, I thought. Shelves weren't even things at all. They were scaffolding for things. They were meant to hold things that were more interesting than they were, to disappear under what they were holding. I mean, cat food was gross and so were chicken nuggets, but at least they were things. Shelves weren't, like, *anything*.

Marianne heard me hesitating. "Look, we have to move forward," she said. "There is nothing wrong with shelves! They're totally inoffensive! Isn't that what you wanted when you said 'neutral'?"

"Well, yes."

"And Boston is really close to Vermont—it will be less expensive to transport them and they'll be up there with Vinnie and Frank sooner."

I took a deep breath and told myself I was having a cognitive distortion and was overly focused on my shipping container house backstory. There were so many things in the world that I didn't even want to hear about, in terms of their backstories. Why was I so focused on this? Did I want to know my Caring bar backstory? No. I didn't care about it. I just wanted to believe that it had something to do with caring, and then I wanted to eat it without thinking, while watching a video of a cat smashing a vase.

"Shelves it is," I said.

17

JACK WAS IN eleventh grade at Chase and would be applying for college next year. His college counselor, Mr. Rudge, wanted to have a chat with me.

I had studiously avoided doing anything at Chase after the PTA debacle. I showed up only when I had to, for parent-teacher conferences or for meetings where I was summoned, like this one.

Mr. Rudge appeared on my screen in a shirt and tie. His video background was set to a tropical island. I could see the fake waves coming up on the fake beach. If I could just carry that background around with me, I thought, I wouldn't have to go to all this trouble getting a beach house. I could be at the beach all the time. Maybe that's what it was like when you were fully alive. Maybe that's what it was like when you had mantra'd "I radiate love" enough so that the mantra wasn't just words anymore. The love you were radiating was real, and it was around you, 24/7, like your own tropical island womb.

"I see you're at the beach, Mr. Rudge!" I exclaimed.

"I can change it to the Death Star if you find it distracting, Mrs. Means," he said, his face somber.

"Oh no, it's fine," I said. No playing, I told myself. This wasn't an architect's office.

Mr. Rudge launched into an explanation of what Jack needed to do for the next year and a half if he wanted to go to "a competitive college."

"Have you visited any colleges yet?" he asked.

I didn't know that was supposed to be my job. I felt my stomach clench. "Not yet," I said.

"Well, eleventh grade is when we tell our kids to start visiting schools and to start thinking about their narratives."

"Their narratives?" I felt my heart rate increase.

"Students need to explain who they are and what they're doing to sell themselves to an admissions team," he said.

I watched as Mr. Rudge flipped through the lengthy question-naire he had given Jack about what kind of college he might like to go to and what he might want to study there. "So, it looks like your son likes writing," he observed. "Has he published anything?"

"In the school lit mag," I said proudly.

"One of our juniors is a poet who has a social media presence with over a million followers," he said, looking at me evenly. "That student has a six-figure book deal already."

I stared at the waves behind Mr. Rudge. I wondered if he actually liked the beach. I bet he didn't.

"You can see how competitive admissions for creative writing students can be," he continued. The leaves in the palm tree behind him were shaking. "Have you looked at the financial-aid forms yet? They're quite comprehensive."

"Oh, I'm good with writing down numbers," I said.

"Well, if you haven't already, you really need to get Jack started thinking about what his hook will be for his college essay."

"Do you have any suggestions?" I asked.

"Does he have any extracurriculars at all? He didn't say much here."

"He's interested in the environment as well as the problem of income inequality," I offered.

"Hmm, well, there's a very well-regarded summer program in Guatemala where he could build houses. But it's very competitive. And rather pricey, of course."

I nodded. Mr. Rudge sat in the breeze, unruffled, as the trees shimmied.

"I'll talk to Jack," I said.

Mr. Rudge kept talking, but I had stopped listening. A few minutes later, I left him on his desert island, hoping just a little that he might get mauled by a passing lion.

18

JACK WAS MOPING over his breakfast in the kitchen. He had had a fight with Betty. I decided not to talk to him about needing to figure out his college backstory yet.

"Have you ever heard that equation about comedy?" I asked him. "Comedy equals truth plus pain?"

"I thought it was comedy equals tragedy plus time," he said, not looking up from his device.

I decided not to say anything else to him about pain, since he was feeling it, but I was thinking about pain. So many factors could be plugged into an equation to equal pain. Zero money could equal pain, for example. But tons of money could also equal pain. Mo' money, mo' problems; I think Mother Teresa said that.

Jerry was in our apartment, cleaning. I got the cash to pay him from my secret bag, which was one of my dad's plastic bags shoved in the back of my T-shirt drawer. I tried to remember to keep the bag relatively full of cash because as part of our disaster preparation we always have a bunch of cash on hand in addition to all the food, medicine, and pet supplies the New York City officials recommend you keep stashed somewhere in your apartment in case of an emergency. I also keep leftover drugs from George's knee surgery in the cash bag, thinking that when the robot uprising happens, and cash means nothing anymore, maybe expired pain meds will help us get a ride through the Midtown Tunnel.

Jerry was in the bathroom, wearing yellow rubber gloves.

"Thanks, Jerry," I said, extending my hand with the cash in it.

"Just put it there," he said, gesturing to the counter.

I never saw Jerry touch the cash. He always told me to set it somewhere and then later, after he left, I'd see the cash was gone. That probably tells you everything you need to know about money right there. But if you want more facts, here are two more I found:

+ 94 percent of one-dollar bills have pneumonia-causing bacteria on them.

+ Almost 80 percent of all dollar bills carry traces of cocaine.

I told Jack another fact: that George and I were on our way to Crashing Sound for a meeting, and that he needed to take care of his sister for the day. We'd be back by dinner, I said. He lifted his eyes from his device long enough to stare at me glumly as he drew a check mark in the air.

I had tried to get a free upgrade on the rental car, but I hadn't spent enough money on my card to earn that reward. So George and I entered the Crashing Sound parking lot in the cheapest compact car that was available. The cars already parked in the lot were far more expensive than ours and didn't have rental car company stickers on them.

We parked on the far side of the lot, away from all the other cars. It was going to be April soon. The sun was out, and the trees had a lemony cast coming into their branches. We walked across the lot, and it was not at all like London in fog. There wasn't a typhoid epidemic. Pickpockets weren't lurking in the shadows, waiting to surprise us by taking our wallets and/or bursting into song. We walked toward the clubhouse, and we were not in a feel-good musical about poor people. We weren't even bad actors. We were just regular, not-rich rich people.

I had dressed for the meeting. I had pulled my hair back in a loose ponytail that I had tied with a black satin ribbon. Very Victorian, I thought. I bought both George and myself new, plain black clothing. There were no words on us—no labels, no logos. I wanted us to be totally unreadable. If we were pots of blacking, we would have been two that a young Charles Dickens had been too tired to paste the labels on. You would just have to look at us and figure out what we were, all by yourself.

We were almost at the clubhouse when Marianne bounded out of the brush like a deer. She was wearing a full-length faux-fur coat and glasses with large red frames. Showtime, I thought.

"Glad I caught you before the meeting! I need to give you these," she said, out of breath. She held out a stack of paper to each of us. "Here are your scripts," she announced.

My mouth dropped open. "You didn't say anything about scripts!"

"I didn't want to scare you," she said, "but these people can be *super* judgy, so I made us scripts for the meeting. All you have to do is follow along!"

"But you said this meeting was just a formality!" I protested.

"*You*, especially!" she said to me, pointing her finger at my chest. "Do not go off script!"

"Don't you trust us to say the right thing?" George asked.

"It's not that I don't trust you," she said, peering at me—me!—over her fiery glasses. "It's that you don't know this community like I do; you don't know the phrases that set them off."

"Yes I do," I said evenly. "'Affordable housing.'"

"Exactly." She grinned at me. "That's why I made you this script."

"Marianne!" I fumed, batting the paper away. "This meeting isn't scripted! It's improv! '*Yes and!*'"

She glared at me. "You have no idea what you're talking about. If you're not going to follow the script, then just don't say anything, OK?" She stomped off into the clubhouse in her high-heeled leather boots.

I was hurt. I was sure that my reputation as a hotheaded bottle thrower had preceded me. How long was it going to take me to live down that stupid mistake?

I followed Marianne inside the clubhouse. It actually looked a lot like Marianne's office: a conference table, chairs, a bunch of files strewn around.

Bea was already sitting there. Two people were sitting at the conference table on either side of her—Leah, who had a smart silver bob that hid most of her face, and Art, an older man in a purple argyle sweater-vest. The vest looked like it had been taken straight from George's pile.

The pile had grown to over a foot tall now. George had also been doing his research. He was well versed in the Scottish labels Pringle and Ballantyne. He could tell you which patterns were produced in which years. He was approaching cashmere-pedia levels of sweater knowledge.

"Nice vest," George said to him when Bea introduced him. "Is it a Pringle?"

"Ballantyne," Art said.

"I could have sworn that shade of lavender was Pringle, from the fall 2002 line," George said.

"Ballantyne," Art repeated stonily.

I didn't want to start the meeting in a tiff about sweater provenance. I grabbed George's hand and pulled him over to sit down beside me.

Bea stood up. "Our third committee member couldn't make it because she's at Pilates," she announced. "So I will be voting in her place. She gave me her proxy."

She got out of this for Pilates?! I was annoyed. Also, I hadn't realized they were actually going to *vote* on our house. I hadn't been the subject of a vote since running for student council in seventh grade. And I had lost, naturally, to a cheerleader with big boobs.

"We have copies of your plans here," Bea said, riffling through the papers I had sent. Leah was studying the materials, her bob falling in a precise angle along her jawline. Art was focused on an insect buzzing in the air. He grabbed at it, then regarded his empty palm, muttering.

"These are very clever plans," Bea said, looking at Marianne. "You call this . . . a modern house?"

"It's modern, yes," Marianne replied.

"Hmmm. You call it a modern house. You can call it whatever you want." Bea smiled slyly at Leah. "But any fool can see that this is a trailer." Bea looked at Leah, who bobbed her bob approvingly.

Marianne growled. "It is *not* a trailer!"

Bea banged her hand on the table. "It *is* a trailer!" she said, leaning toward Marianne. "It's metal, it's a box. It's a *trailer!*"

"It's a *container*," yelled Marianne, half rising out of her chair.

"*Trailer!*" yelled Bea.

Art's head had tipped forward so his chin sat on one of his purple diamonds. He was dozing. I felt my face getting hot.

"I am an architect," Marianne said, softening her voice and spreading her hands out imploringly. "I know what a trailer is. And this is not."

"I am not an architect," Bea replied, brandishing her device. "But I can tell you that according to this, a trailer, also known as *a mobile home*, is"—she read from her screen—" 'any prefabricated structure built in a factory and transported to a site'! Now, how did you say you were getting your house to our neighborhood? In a flatbed truck?" Her eyes twinkled.

"Yes, but—" Marianne began.

"You seem like such nice people," Leah interrupted. "But I'm sorry, this neighborhood is *not* a trailer park." She swung her bob.

I closed my eyes. "Only poor people see obstacles," I mantra'd to myself.

"I call for a vote," Bea announced.

"I second," Leah said.

"All in favor of the trailer?" Bea cried.

Art snorted again.

"*Art!*" Bea yelled. "We're voting!"

He raised his head quickly. "Yes!"

"*No*, Art!" Bea groaned. "The question is, are you in favor of the trailer?"

"Oh! No!" Art corrected himself.

"All opposed, then?"

Art's, Leah's, and Bea's hands shot up.

A murderous rage bubbled up in me, and I couldn't contain it any longer. "It's not a trailer, it's my *home!*" I cried, picking up my device and throwing it in the general direction of Bea's head.

As soon as the device left my fingertips, my perception changed. I saw it fly in slow motion, hitting the clubhouse wall with a thunk, and then I saw everyone at the meeting as if I had X-ray vision, and I was thinking, isn't it funny how ribs are like shelves that people carry inside their own shipping container selves, and look at the important job they're doing there: protecting our tender hearts.

All the lights in the clubhouse went off, and the clubhouse became a container ship sinking down to the bottom of the ocean.

I reached out to George and held his hand as we swam out the door. A giant wave carried us up and over the expensive cars in the parking lot to the beach and deposited us on the sand.

We lay there, breathing hard. Marianne ambled over to us. She took our hands and pulled us up, like she was a sports mascot and we were big-league players who had fallen on the basketball court.

"C'mon," she said. "Let's go get something to eat."

Slush

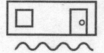

1

I GOT BACK IN the rental car with George. We followed Marianne to a lobster place. The GPS didn't work well in The Springs because the wireless service was so bad.

The air in the car was tense. I was ashamed I had relapsed on my throwing habit. I knew that George was going to tell me that whatever therapy I was doing wasn't working. I had already messaged Alice for an extra session.

I was also furious with Bea. Sure, it's not like *I* was seeking to live among poor people and their trailers, either. But I didn't walk around enforcing rules saying people who lived in trailers couldn't come near me. It wasn't *my* fault that I didn't happen to know any people who lived in trailers. Except for my mom's cousins, and when I was growing up, we never visited "those people," as my mother called them.

I stole a glance at George. I didn't know what he was thinking. Probably he was relieved: no beach house for us.

"Look, there's the sign," George said.

I had to dip my head to see what he was looking at. It was a sixty-foot-tall electronic billboard, flashing above the overgrown grass. The top of the sign was adorned with the seal of the Shinnecock Indian Nation. Below it, strobing, colored lights spelled out: OLIVER! ON BROADWAY! TIX ON SALE NOW!!

"The Shinnecock people call that their monument," he said. "Folks in Southampton say it's an eyesore and have been trying to tear it down. But the Shinnecock are getting a ton of advertising revenue for it."

"Good for them," I said.

"I saw in the paper that they want to build a casino here, too," George added.

"Where?" I asked.

"Here," he said, gesturing toward the scrub as we pulled into the lobster shack parking lot. "This is the Shinnecock reservation."

"This?!" I cried, getting out of the car, my feet crunching on the gravel parking lot.

"Well, not *here*," George clarified, closing the car door. "Over *there*." He waved his arm toward the area beyond the lot, covered with tall grass, where a small wooden sign read SHINNECOCK NATION: TRESPASSERS KEEP OUT.

"The reservation doesn't look like it's on a prime parcel of land," I observed as we crunched across the lot toward the restaurant.

"Well, do you think they were given waterfront? Hell no," George said.

"Is there even water access from here?" I was squinting, trying to see into the distance.

George craned his neck. "I don't see any."

"It's like when a beach hotel says a room is 'ocean view.' It means you can see the water from the window if you're sitting at the right angle. But if you want to see the water unobstructed, you need to spring for what's called 'oceanfront.'" I was happy to be able to expound on a subject I knew something about.

George and I joined Marianne, who was already sitting at a table. "I ordered the lobster special for you two already," she said. "Trust me, it's great."

I was tired of trusting Marianne. I watched her as she examined her silverware for any crud the dishwasher had missed.

"This place is owned by the Shinnecock Indian Nation, so I like to come here to support it. You know, the majority of people on the reservation are living below the poverty level," she said.

I didn't often get so close to the places where people were suffering like that. Sure, I had an app on my phone that showed me exactly where people were getting assaulted on West Twenty-Seventh Street, but that didn't really count, because my neighborhood was still in Manhattan, and Manhattan, if you had to equate it to a hotel room, is still clinging to the title of America's Executive Suite.

A waitress brought out the lobster Marianne had ordered for us. I admired the shiny red shells as I tied my crinkly plastic lobster bib behind my neck.

We tackled the beasts with our utensils. The shells cracked noisily.

"So, you had a real Hamptons welcome, didn't you?" Marianne said finally, digging into the carcass with her tiny fork. "Don't be discouraged, these meetings can get very dramatic sometimes."

"I'll say," George said, chewing.

"The important thing is that you stay focused. You need to put the house up regardless of this meeting. You know that, right?" She held her fork with its skewered lobster bit poised in midair.

What the hell is it with architects? I wondered. They invest everything, emotionally, in the structure they've designed, and then they fight for its life, as if the structure in all its glorious detail is a stand-in for themselves. And they have to battle for its existence with their hands tied behind their backs, because they can't will it into the world by using any of their own money. They can't pay for it themselves; they have to *be paid* for it. They just have to be completely, psychotically dogged about this shepherding of their stand-in self into existence, with no resources other than their charm and some marks on paper. And they can't say they're finished with it until they can touch it, until it is a solid thing in the world. They're as bad as writers, I thought.

"You told us it was definitely going to be approved, no problem!" I fumed.

"I know, I know," she said dismissively. "But I'm telling you, this is just a silly protocol! You can still go ahead and build it. They can't sue!"

"Because they have no money?" George asked, looking at her skeptically.

"Yes!" she said triumphantly.

George sighed and turned his head to look at a lime-green Lamborghini with gull-wing doors rumbling into the lobster shack parking lot.

Marianne veered the conversation back to the house's construction. She told us that Vinnie and Frank had received the formerly shelf-filled containers at their warehouse in Vermont and were almost done putting in the windows. Once that was done, the process would move fairly quickly. They would need four to six weeks max to get the finishes and flooring in, and then the containers would be ready to go.

"If we still want them, that is," George added.

"Of course you still want them!" Marianne said. I caught a glimpse of pink lobster meat between her teeth.

I wasn't sure what to say because I didn't know what the alternative would be. Just leaving some half-finished container house up in Vermont in giant garbage bags on the side of the road, the way some people ditch newborn puppies?

Marianne looked at me. "I think we need to go over your budget again."

"We're never going to put this house up, Marianne," George interjected. "But if you want to go ahead, I'll humor you."

Marianne went ahead, fixing her gaze on me. I supposed I was the weak link in the system.

"If you want to keep the pool, you're going to need to let go of that multicolored pool lighting system you asked me to price out for you," Marianne began.

"Oh, for Chrissakes," George said. "That lighting setup is ridiculous."

I exhaled. I knew George didn't care about swimming in a heated, psychedelic womb like I did.

"Even if we *do* get a house built someday," George said, "we don't need a pool! The ocean is a five-minute walk!"

I took a breath. "A pool is a must," I declared.

George made a face. I took another bite of lobster and looked out on a Bentley and a Land Rover awkwardly square dancing as they attempted to park.

"OK," Marianne said. "It will be an unheated pool. We'll get the pool guy to start digging it, and Stan will work on installing the well and the septic tank." Stan was our contractor. "You're going to have to do something for me, though, Shelly."

"What?"

"I need you to reach out to Bea and make peace."

I felt my stomach drop like a raccoon falling down a chimney. "Wait, what?!"

"You need to meet with her, in person, and apologize," Marianne said sternly.

"What are you talking about? I am not a good peacemaker! Were you even at that meeting just now?!"

"That's why it has to be you," Marianne said calmly, adjusting her lobster bib. She smiled slyly. "You made your bed, I think the expression goes?"

2

"YOU HAVE TO get a handle on this throwing habit, Shelly," George said, as we got back in the rental car after lunch.

"I *know*," I said defensively. "I've already been in touch with Alice."

"Do you really think she's helping?"

"Of course," I said. "It's just not an easy habit to break."

"If this continues, you need to try some other strategies," he said, pulling onto the L.I.E.

I sat in the car and listened to the new sad-song playlist George had made.

As we were passing Ronkonkoma, George suddenly had an idea: we should sell the land immediately, with the architectural plans, as a package. That way we could get reimbursed for the land and also recoup at least some, if not all, of the money we had paid Marianne for her marks on paper.

"But that solution doesn't leave us with a house!" I argued.

"Yes, but it does leave us with *some* money rather than *no* money," George replied. "The only problem is, I don't know if we even own the plans like that, as something we could sell. Could you call Tim and ask him about it?"

My shoulders tightened at the idea, but I said I would make the call. As soon as we were home, though, I made a different call, to Alice.

"Good lord, that sounds awful," she said, when I told her about the meeting.

I could hear her beeping her car horn. "Hold on a minute," she said, "I'm pulling over so I can look something up for you."

I waited as I heard her engine quiet down.

"I want you to call a friend of mine. She's very special and I only send very dear clients to her. I'm sending you her info now. Call her and tell her I sent you."

I looked at my device. "Cat," the contact read. There was a long phone number attached to it, as if Cat, whoever they were, was very far away.

3

TWO DAYS LATER, Darby walked in the door of the apartment. I had been dreading her coming because I had to tell her we were letting her go. George and I had discussed what we could cut from our expenses, and that was one thing we agreed on: we didn't need a dog walker.

Darby leaned down to pet Twix. I could see elaborate leather cuffs peeking out from the wrists of her hoodie.

"Are those leather handcuffs?"

"They're not handcuffs," she said, standing up and shaking her arms. "They're handcuff-*inspired*." She held them out for me to admire. "My harness design didn't get a very good grade in accessories class, so I'm trying these," she continued. "They're meant to call attention to the bondage of women sex workers and the need for Americans to decriminalize that work."

I was too nervous about delivering my I-have-to-fire-you speech to listen closely. "Darby, I have to tell you something," I began, in a serious tone.

"Has Twix been talking to you about Walter lately, too?"

I wasn't sure I had heard her correctly.

"Your friend Walter, the painter," Darby explained. "Twix keeps saying the market for his work is going to go through the roof."

"Twix is an art market prognosticator?"

"I'm just passing along what she said," Darby replied snippily.

"I don't have the money to buy art," I said quickly. "Speaking of which, Darby, I am sorry, but I have to let you go today. We just can't afford any extras right now, including dog walking."

She looked at me, surprised. "Oh, I'm sorry to hear that!"

She bent down, hiding her face, and picked up Twix to kiss her on the head.

"I know Twix loves you," I said miserably. "I hope this is only temporary."

"I'll be happy to pick up the work again anytime," she said, setting Twix down. "I've enjoyed working with you."

I felt awful as I handed her the envelope with her cash inside it. She took it and turned to go back out the door.

"Darby, I have to ask you for the key back," I said uncomfortably.

She blushed, retrieving the key from her ring.

"Thanks," I said, as she passed it to me.

Darby avoided my gaze. "See you later, Twix," she said, closing the door behind her.

I sighed, grateful that moment was over. I reminded myself that it was undeniably a ridiculous luxury to pay for a dog walker when I was right here to walk the dog. I genuinely liked Darby, though, and felt guilty about letting her go. I would miss her, as superficial as our relationship was. I just had a feeling about her: she was going places.

4

CAT, IT TURNED out, was a "financial psychic" who specialized in helping people with money problems. I texted and told her that Alice had sent me. We scheduled a time to meet.

I had never been to a regular psychic, let alone a financial one. I wasn't sure what to expect. When I connected with Cat online, I saw that she was a little younger than Alice, with light-brown skin and a dark-brown updo. She wore a white collared shirt like the ones authors wear for their photos. I asked her where she was in the world.

"Buenos Aires," she said, with a slight Spanish accent, "but I also have a place on East Fourteenth Street."

"Ah, a fellow New Yorker," I said.

Cat smiled as she explained that she would be using a tarot deck she had made herself. She was a painter, but she supported herself as a day trader. She did these readings on the side.

I sat and watched as she spread the cards out on a table. I admired their backs. The image was taken from one of her own paintings, she told me. It was a stack of cash, but not painted in a colorful, enticing way, like Walter's images. This view of money was more foreboding—in black and white, with heavy lines, like a woodcut by Escher.

"Look me in the eyes, please," Cat said.

I looked at her on the screen. It was uncomfortable. I felt like she had her hand in my pocket.

She sat back. "Feel free to ask me anything you want to ask about money."

I was surprised. I thought she would be telling me things about money, not that I would be asking things. But I did have something I wanted to know about, of course, which was my beach house. I spilled my beach house acquisition narrative for her in the shortest form possible.

She smiled absentmindedly as I talked. Maybe she heard problems like this all the time. I was just another person trying to buy something they couldn't really afford.

"Is that all?" she asked, when I finished.

"Well, I don't really understand money," I confessed.

"Economics is just a story told by so-called experts," she said, as she shuffled the cards. "Now, look: I am going to draw three cards for you. I want you to tell me the thoughts and images that come up for you with these cards."

I nodded, but I was thinking: Wasn't she supposed to be the card reader, not me? This felt a lot like designing my own beach house at the architect's office.

The first card she flipped looked a lot like a baseball card, except instead of a portrait of a baseball player, it was Karl Marx.

"What does this card make you think of?" Cat asked.

"That Marx is one of the so-called experts telling me the story of economics?"

"This isn't a quiz," Cat chided. "There is no wrong answer."

I felt myself blush. She turned over the second card.

"What's that a picture of?" I asked, squinting.

"A woman masturbating under a waterfall. How do these two cards relate to each other, to you?"

This was by far the most difficult story problem I had ever been assigned in my life. "Karl Marx was hot?" I tried.

"Well, some think so," she said. She pulled the last card and showed it to me: the Ace of Spades.

"Well, that card I know." I smiled. "Because I am a Motörhead fan."

Cat stared intently at the card. I told myself that from here on in, I was going to conduct myself how I imagined a gambler would. I would sit silently, with a perfectly straight face, until I knew when to walk away and when to run.

"So what do you think?" she asked, putting the ace back in the deck and shuffling the cards.

I threw it back at her, gambler-style. "What *is* money, again?" I asked.

"Money makes some things easier," she said. "That's all."

I wasn't sure I believed that. Plus, she hadn't answered *my* question. "I thought you were going to give me some guidance on my beach house drama," I said.

"That's what you wanted?"

"Yes!"

She shuffled the cards and then peered at me intently. "You know, *you* can make a lot of money," she said.

"Oh, *sure*." I smirked.

"I see it in your future," she said. "You're going to make a ton of money."

I puckered my mouth like I had tasted something sour.

"What's the block?" she asked. "Why don't you want to make money?"

"Of course I want to make money!" I sputtered.

"Are you sure? Close your eyes," she commanded.

It wasn't what a high roller would have done, but I did what she said.

"Why not?" she prodded. "What would happen if you made a lot of money?"

I kept my eyes closed. "Um, I would be participating in a system that confers no value on childcare and other care work routinely shouldered by women, and that's work that I believe is hugely important and valuable?"

"Mm-hmm. And what do you get by not participating in that system?"

"Ah, a feeling like, I'm sort of protesting it? By, like, balking? Like *Bartleby, the Scrivener*?"

"Melville!" she exclaimed. "Good. Also, my dear, you should try not to uptalk so much. You don't need to diffuse your power like that."

I opened my eyes and looked down. My heart was racing. I wasn't used to being seen this clearly.

When I looked back at the screen, she was holding up a book. Her face was on the cover. The title was *Bitches Get Riches: The Life and Times of Cat, the World's Greatest Financial Psychic*.

"I suggest you get my memoir," she said, waving it at me. "There is a ton of basic financial advice in it. Plus, you can read about my terrible childhood." She smiled brightly.

"I'll look for it," I said politely. I didn't want to tell her I was a former English major who only read the great works of literature. But she was an appealing salesperson, that's for sure. I decided to lob her my most urgent question.

"Cat, what should someone do if they want to be more fully alive?"

I watched as she looked down at her hands. She spread her fingers out in front of her and flexed them, as if she were a concert pianist.

"If you want to be more fully alive, you can't be running away to your beach house all the time," she said finally, looking up at me.

"That's not what it looks like on social media," I countered.

She didn't respond to that. Instead, she looked at the clock. "That's all the time I have now," she said.

Figures, I thought. "What do I owe you?" I asked.

"Nothing," she said. "This is my gift. I give it away."

I was surprised. I wasn't accustomed to people giving me things for free. I mean, I was used to getting free hotel rooms, but those were a reward. I had to do something to get them.

"Thank you," I said.

I had one more question, though. I asked Cat how she knew Alice.

"She didn't tell you?" She smiled demurely. "I'm her ex."

5

I ARRANGED FOR A meeting with Bea for two days later. I asked her by email if I might stop by her house to apologize in person for my outburst. I was sure she would say no. I would be so happy if she said no.

She said yes. But rather than meet at her house, she suggested we meet for a walk on the beach.

I didn't tell anyone about the meeting except George. I didn't want to have to confess to Alice or anyone else if it was a disaster.

"You're going to do great," George said, giving me a kiss as I headed out the door.

"HA HA HA," I said, mimicking his voice-over warm-up. Then I drove to the beach with my coffee in the cupholder, blasting heavy metal to psyche myself up.

As I pulled into the beach parking lot two a half hours later, I saw Bea standing stiffly at the edge of the sand in a gray tracksuit. Her little Doodle was with her, on a leash. I wished I had brought Twix with me. She would know how to behave.

Bea saw me, then bent down to let her dog off the leash, to run freely on the sand.

"Hey, what's your dog's name?" I asked breathlessly, as I caught up to her.

"Pi," she said.

"Pie?"

"No, Pi. Like 3.1415 . . . I'm a former math teacher."

I was so nervous about getting my apology out I couldn't think straight. I tried to focus on the damp sand shifting under my boots as we walked. I took a deep breath and thought: I radiate love. Then I blurted out, "I'm really sorry about throwing my phone in your direction at the meeting."

"In my direction?!" Bea glared at me.

"*At* you," I clarified. "I threw my phone *at* you."

"Yes, you did," she said. Pi had stopped to sniff at a dead bluefish. "You're lucky it didn't hit me in the face," she added.

"I know," I said sheepishly.

We walked in silence. Was she accepting my apology?

"Where are you from, Shelly?" she asked.

"Originally? Minneapolis."

"Never been there," she said. "I've lived in Springs all my life."

"You're very lucky," I said, picking up a Creamsicle-toned shell to save for Clementine.

"It's not that easy to make a living out here, you know," she said. "I worked for twenty-five years for the Springs School District, and my husband worked for the town until he passed two years ago."

"I'm sorry for your loss," I said. I felt like we were backtracking, covering all the niceties that hadn't gotten said at the meeting.

"The hardest thing about living here so long," she said, as we approached the pier, "is seeing all the ways we've sold out our town to rich people."

I wasn't sure if she thought I was a rich person or not. I had assumed *she* was the rich person.

"So when rich people come into the area with their big ideas, we have to try to slow them down," she said, sitting down at the edge of the pier as Pi sat in the shade underneath it.

Was I a rich person? Was my house a big idea?

"Our Home Aesthetics Committee may seem silly to you," she continued, "but it's our only firewall to keep the neighborhood from going to hell with crazy rich-people ideas."

"But you accused me of being a poor person with poor-person ideas!" I sputtered, taking a seat beside her on the pier. "You accused me of trying to turn your neighborhood into a trailer park!"

"I know," she said calmly. "Because it's the extremes. The extremes are the problem. Did you know that a guy recently tried to buy five separate houses in Silver Sound in order to build one giant mansion plus a public museum for his vintage pinball machines?"

"Really?" That *was* a crazy idea.

"The Home Aesthetics Committee is how we are able to get ahead of situations like that. We're just trying to hold on to a middle here!" She banged her hand on the pier for emphasis. "A *real* middle! Not a fake middle where someone *thinks* they're in the middle because they can't afford a second home!"

My mind was racing like I was doing a math problem with a timer on. I had thought *I* was in the real middle. But if Bea was in the real middle, did that mean I was in the upper? But how could that be when I just had to fire my dog walker?

I watched Pi chase a seagull. I wondered if either of them talked.

"My house is all I have," Bea said softly. "It's my savings. I'm leaving it to our son."

"I understand," I said. "I'm not rich, either."

"Of course you're not," she scoffed. "You're just another striver from the city coming to Springs."

I didn't know what to say to that. I never thought of myself as a striver. After all, I "didn't work." And I wanted so little, it seemed! But I could see how she thought so.

"What makes a person rich isn't a beach house in East Hampton," she continued. "What makes a person rich is never having to work again because of generational wealth."

I sat there, wondering if this meeting had been worth the trouble. Pi came over and sat by me. She licked my hand. A dog in the world liked me. That was something, anyway.

"OK, Bea," I said. "I hear you on all this. But I still want to build my container house. One container house doesn't mean the area will be overrun with container houses. And even if it did mean that, that wouldn't be so bad. It's a nice house designed by an amazing architect!"

"I do admire your architect," Bea admitted, rummaging in her pocket to pull out a dog treat for Pi. "She's sharp."

I was gratified to hear Bea acknowledge some respect for Marianne after their clash. I watched the ocean sparkle.

"I can make the committee vote happen for you," Bea said, giving Pi her treat. "Would you be willing to make a donation to the Silver Sound Homeowner's Association?"

I was so grateful for my old PTA job then. I had learned so much there, from Kevin, that Cash Winehouse guy. I knew just what to say.

"How much?" I asked.

She said some numbers.

"Great," I said. "And in turn you give us the green light for our house, and then someone will write something nice about it in the Silver Sound newsletter."

"Of course," she said, as she stood back up. We began to walk back to the parking lot.

We got about halfway there when she suddenly warned, "But if you ever throw anything at me again, I am calling the cops!"

"I won't," I said seriously.

"And let me tell you, everyone who works in this town—from the police to the town hall—is my *very good friend*."

I watched Pi loping ahead of us, wagging her tail, happy.

"Mistakes are how we learn," I said, looking at her with a shy grin.

6

A WEEK LATER, BETTY walked out the door of our apartment on West Twenty-Seventh Street as George walked in. They were like two container ships barely managing to pass each other without incident in the Suez Canal.

"Three cashmere sweaters!" George announced, throwing a bag on the table.

George's sweater pile was growing at a pretty good clip. It must have been two feet high now.

"I thought you went on an audition today," I said.

"I did."

"How'd it go?"

He put on the voice-over voice: "Feel depressed? You're not alone. Depression is the leading cause of disability in the United States."

I raised my eyebrows. "What's that an ad for, depression?"

"No, it's a public service announcement."

"Does that mean you won't get paid for it?"

"I don't even know if I got the gig yet! But yes, it's nonpaying."

"Hmm," I said, looking down.

"I figured it would be good exposure," he explained, opening a can of Loving seltzer with a hiss and pop.

"But don't you think that being the depression voice might mean that you won't get cast as the sandwich voice?" I asked. "People don't want to eat depression."

"I know," he said. "But I can't think like that."

"Like what?"

"I can't strategize like that! I'm just trying to find a job!"

I studied him as he gulped seltzer, then burped. "I'm going to give you my vision board," I said. It was almost empty now that Marianne had stripped my house bare.

Jerry came down the hallway humming a show tune and holding an armful of clean sheets. I realized I needed to pay him. I went to my secret bag in the bedroom to get cash. Twix followed me, sitting down at my feet as I reached into the bag.

"You should really pay Jerry more," Twix said.

I looked at her. "Is that all you ever think about? Money?"

"No, it's all *you* ever think about," she said.

"That's not true," I said. "I think about lots of other things."

"Like what? Beach houses?"

"Yes," I snapped, glaring at her.

She snorted and looked away.

It was hard to accept that my dog thought I was an idiot. Your cat was the one who was supposed to think you were an idiot.

"I think about you a lot, Twix," I said, stooping down to pet her. "I love you."

"Whatever," she said, rolling over on her back so I could give her a belly rub. "Are you going to decide that I'm too expensive, and then send me away, like you did with Darby?"

7

WE NEEDED TO make a little donation to the Silver Sound Homeowner's Association, I told George, and everything would be fine. We could go ahead and build the house. The only problem now was that we needed the money to build the house.

"Shelly, we've already been over this," George groused. "I'm not working! I have zero gigs! We don't have the money to go ahead with your nutty house project right now! The only thing you should be doing about this beach house is calling Tim to see if we can recoup our money by selling the land and the plans together! Did you do that yet?"

"No," I confessed.

"Please do that," he said, and went to walk the dog.

While he was out, I called Tim. I could hear a mechanical whirring in the background when I got him. A rowing machine, I guessed.

"Why are you asking me this?" Tim complained, panting, after I asked him George's question about selling the land and house plans together.

"Because you're the lawyer?"

"No, I mean, why aren't you building your house now instead of asking me these questions?!"

I began telling them the story about the meeting. He cut me off.

"Oh for fuck's sake, do you even remember what I told you about this housing association nonsense?"

"No?"

"They're broke! They have bigger problems than you and your trailer!"

"It's not a trailer, Tim!" I was hurt.

"I don't care what it is! Just put it up already! I can't wait to see it when it's done!"

"But, Tim, George isn't making any money," I said.

I heard the whirring stop. "What the hell happened?!"

I was surprised by how surprised he was. Maybe this didn't happen much in his lawyer/shaman circles. "He's not working," I said. "He hasn't gotten a gig in months."

"People don't make money," Tim told me, suddenly serious. "Money makes money."

I hadn't heard that mantra yet.

"Listen, here's what we'll do." Tim spoke fast. "I'll set you up with my guy to get a loan at a good rate. That way you can at least get the house up. You can use it as an income stream until you get this employment situation sorted out."

On some level I was shocked to hear that I wasn't going to be penalized for not having money. "Is that even legal?" I asked.

Tim made a scoffing sound. "Did you grow up poor?"

This did seem to be the million-dollar question lately. "I don't think so?"

"I ask because when you're poor in America and you miss some credit card payments, you get your credit card taken away. And then you can't find an apartment to rent because you have a blotch on your credit report. And then you're unhoused, and once that happens, you're only further punished, and obviously, that's traumatizing," he said.

"That didn't happen to me when I was a kid," I said, thinking how that wasn't even Dickensian, it was Kafkaesque.

"Well, I will work with you so that that doesn't happen now, either," he said.

"OK," I said, like I understood. But what I was really starting to understand was why people with money never took having no money seriously.

8

"DID YOU TALK to Mr. Rudge about your backstory for college applications yet?" I asked Jack a day later, when he emerged from his room for breakfast.

He grabbed a cereal bowl and the box of chocolate Pluck and sat down at the table. I followed him with the red carton of milk. His black hair flopped into his eyes. "Wasn't my backstory supposed to be my good grades?" he asked.

"You need more than that these days, according to Mr. Rudge." I reminded myself that I still needed to fill out the financial-aid forms. Maybe all this financial strife would somehow work in Jack's favor. "Do you still want to focus on schools that offer creative writing?" I asked him.

He nodded.

"Did you know there's a poet at your school who already has a book deal?"

"Oh god, Mom," he said, crunching the Pluck. "That's Brianna. Her dad is the head of a publishing house."

I sighed. "Well, Mr. Rudge says you need a hook for your essay."

He continued crunching. Under his floppy forelock I couldn't tell if he was thinking about it or not.

"What about spending the summer building houses in Guatemala?" I ventured.

"Mom!"

"Well, do you have any thoughts for something you can write about? You were so good at outlining your novel."

He stood up abruptly and brought the bowl to the sink and dumped the rest of the cereal out. "This stuff tastes awful," he said.

I knew that already.

"Maybe you can get an internship with Marianne," I offered.

"Who's Marianne?"

"Our architect! The woman who's working on our shipping container beach house!"

"How is that going to give me a creative writing backstory?"

"Helloooo!" I called, exasperated. "You could write about sustainable architecture! Aren't you interested in eco-friendliness? Affordability?"

"Mom, I haven't wanted to say anything to you about this because I don't want to harsh on your dreams, but containers are gross. The ships that carry them are environmental hazards created solely to meet America's bloated consumer habits."

I felt prickly. It's not that I didn't care about the environment, of course I did. I just cared a little more about my eco-friendly beach house.

"Jack, don't look a gift shipping container in the mouth! You need a story for your college essay. What are you going to write to sell yourself?"

He stood there, holding his device. "Would I have to leave town to do the internship with Marianne?"

I knew he didn't want to be separated from Betty. "Well, Marianne's office is a lot closer than Guatemala."

"I guess I'll talk to her about it," he said.

9

THERE WAS NOW a multicolored, three-foot-high stack of Salvation Army cashmere sweaters on a table in the middle of our living room on West Twenty-Seventh Street. It had taken a while, but George had managed to construct a sweater monument.

If a sweater was on the monument, it meant it had already been through George's sweater triage: it had been cleaned, mended, or both. It was now ready to be photographed, put online, and sold.

Occasionally I would peel a sweater off the top of the pile and put it on, causing George to scowl and tell me to "quit wearing the merch." Still, I wore the merch. A giant stack of cashmere sweaters is like a pile of puppies in a puppy store window. Irresistible.

I was wearing a lemon-yellow cardigan—a sunny, old-man sweater—when George and I finally came to an agreement about the beach house. And by "came to an agreement," I mean that my beloved life partner finally bought into my beach house sales pitch.

I began by telling George about Tim's proposal that we get a loan and then build the house in order to rent it.

George looked down at his feet in a way that reminded me of Cat looking down at her hands. "You're determined to break me down on this, aren't you," he said.

I sometimes forgot, busy as I was trying not to throw drinking vessels, what a gentle person George was. I felt a wave of tenderness. "I'm not trying to break you down, George," I said quietly.

"What do you want from me, then?" he asked.

"I want you to believe in this story with me," I said.

"What story? The one about our having a beach house?"

"The one about our being happy there, as a family," I said.

"I'm happy *here, now,*" he said. "In our too-small apartment on West Twenty-Seventh Street."

"Well, what do you want me to do, then? Should I just give up this house idea?"

He sighed. "I want you to be happy," he said.

I hugged him.

He kissed my forehead. "Also, I want to go to the Boxy."

10

THE NEXT DAY, I called Marianne to tell her we were back on with our plans. She wasn't put off by our stopping and starting. She went through the timeline with me.

Vinnie and Frank and two other drivers would load the four finished containers onto four flatbed trucks. They would drive one full day from Vermont and then they would park the trucks at a rest stop near our tick farm overnight. The next morning, very early, they would get up and drive the trucks to our land, where there were now four concrete pillars on which to set the containers, courtesy of our contractor, Stan.

The trucks would meet Stan and Stan's team there, and then a specially contracted crane would lift the containers off the trucks, onto the pillars, in their two-by-two stack. And then Stan and his workers would swarm in like bees and seal it all up and connect it to the electrical and plumbing that they had installed, so we could go into our house and turn on the lights and flush the toilets.

"It will be like a modern-day barn raising," Marianne had said, which was surely a fiction, but if you were going to make a story about the way a house could go up, why not make it a happy story, with the community joyfully coming together, rather than having a bitter meeting and an argument.

The next morning, a Sunday, George was up early, eating breakfast.

"Our beach house still has no name," I said to him. It was the first time I had said it out loud like that to George: our beach house.

"So it'll be the house with no name," he said, looking at his device. "'Cause there ain't no one for to give you no pain.'"

"That's 'A Horse with No Name,'" I corrected him, pouring my coffee.

"We should just keep the old name you had for the house," he said. "The Tin Can."

"Don't you think that's mocking it?" I sat down beside him with my coffee in a mug Clementine had bought me for Mother's Day that read BE THE PERSON YOUR DOG THINKS YOU ARE.

He put down his device and stirred more sugar in his coffee. "Maybe a little. But in a nice way. Like a form of endearment. Endearment is love. It's a small thing you do with great love."

We both knew he was quoting Mother Teresa. I don't know why I found his crush on her so annoying. Probably the same reason he would find my going to a financial psychic annoying.

"You think that's what Mother Teresa meant when she said to do small things with great love?" I scoffed. "Name your beach house?"

George looked hurt. We began arguing over what it meant to do a small thing with great love. It got pretty heated for 8:00 a.m. The kids were still sleeping, so we moved the argument to our bedroom, where we continued arguing by having sex.

Later, Clementine came into our bedroom rubbing her eyes, wearing the white bunny cosplay outfit she had asked me to buy her. "Why were you guys yelling?" she asked.

"Here, honey, I made something special for breakfast," I said, getting up off the bed.

I went to get her a croissant. The plate was empty. There had been three croissants sitting there.

I looked around for Twix. It wasn't like her to eat food off the table, but it also wasn't like me to leave a full plate unattended for so long.

Twix wasn't in the kitchen or living room. I began to panic. I ran around the apartment, calling her name. Finally, I heard a strange sound and found her behind the curtains in the living room, vomiting.

Clementine was hovering. "Is it an emergency?" she asked hopefully.

"Yes," I said, grabbing the dog carrier from the hall closet. "I'm taking Twix to the vet."

"I want to come with you," she said.

I scooped Twix into a bath towel and put her in the carrier as George handed me my device. "Come on, then!"

Clementine flew out the apartment door with me in her bunny outfit and flip-flops. She could have been a furry going to Comic-Con but I didn't bother telling her to change. We stood on the sidewalk on Twenty-Seventh Street as I frantically waved for a cab.

As the cab pulled up and we crawled inside, I realized that the vet's office was closed. I directed the cabbie to the animal urgent care I had walked past many times but never visited. In retrospect, it was good I'd never been there before, because I was blissfully ignorant of how high the bill would be later.

I walked in expecting the chaos of an ER and was surprised to find that we were the only ones in the waiting area. The attendant led us to an exam room, which contained a steel table large enough for a horse. I wondered if anyone in Manhattan had ever brought their horse to this urgent care. Maybe a Central Park carriage driver.

I pulled Twix out of her carrier and set her on the horse table in her filthy vomit-and-diarrhea-covered towel. I sat beside her in a plastic chair. Clementine sat beside me.

The doctor came in and greeted us briskly. I marveled at her promptness. Our pediatrician regularly kept us waiting for forty-five minutes in a room not even half this size. I wondered how bad it would be to bring Clementine here in an emergency as I explained to the vet what happened.

"What kind of chocolate was in the croissants?" she asked, as she listened to Twix's breathing.

"Dark chocolate," I said. "They were from Le Pain."

"Dark chocolate contains 130 milligrams of theobromine per ounce," she said. "So if she ate even two ounces, she is well over the twenty milligrams of theobromine per pound of her weight that we consider the threshold for poisoning."

Clementine patted Twix gently as the vet picked Twix up in the filthy towel. "We're going to take her," she said, hurrying out the door and avoiding my eyes. "I'll call you when we have an update."

I wanted to say goodbye to Twix, but her eyes were closed and she seemed unaware we had handed her over. Clementine and I went back to the lobby. I told Clementine I needed the restroom. I closed the door behind me as I stood over the sink and cried. How could I have failed to protect Twix, my rock?!

I splashed cold water on my face and looked in the mirror at my splotched face and grotty clothes. I should be thinking of Clementine's feelings now, I thought, not my own.

I came out of the bathroom and found Clementine looking improbably elegant in her bunny outfit. She had availed herself of the hot chocolate pods in the waiting room coffeemaker and was spilling hot chocolate nonchalantly on her white, fake fur. Maybe all those disaster books she read weren't so bad for her after all, I thought, as I sat down and hugged her. She was comfortable in a crisis, anyway.

11

AS SOON AS we got home, I got into the bathtub. I dropped one of Clementine's glitter bath bombs in the steamy water. I set my device on the rim of the tub so I could answer it, in case the vet called. My device looked like a frog hovering at the edge of a pond. I was tempted to push it into the water, as if that would solve all my problems.

George knocked on the door.

"I'm bathing," I growled.

"I know," he said. He opened the door a crack then came in and sat on the edge of the tub.

"This would never have happened if we hadn't been arguing," I said miserably.

"Dogs eat weird stuff," he said. "It's not your fault."

I put my wet hands over my eyes and leaned back in the tub. "If Twix dies, George, I will never have another animal again. It's too hard."

"What's too hard?"

"It's too hard to love something that dies of something so stupid."

"Everything dies of something stupid," he said.

"Life is stupid," I said.

"You're not stupid," he said. "You're a person who loves your dog. That is the least stupid thing I ever heard."

"If she pulls through this . . ." I started, and then I began to sniffle.

"If she pulls through this, you will be grateful," he said. "And that will be a good thing for you to feel, for a change."

Summer

TWIX SURVIVED.

"Twix, *why* did you eat the croissants?" I asked her. She was on my lap in the cab, after I picked her up from urgent care.

"I wanted to know what they were," she replied sheepishly.

"Well, I hope you've learned something," I chided. "Never eat anything off the table."

She shook herself and then glared at me. "Why does it have to be me who learns?! Why don't *you* learn something for once? You've made a zillion mistakes and you never learn from any of them! Why don't you learn that humans and animals and land and water are all connected? Why don't you learn that you have to share? Why don't you learn that you have to change the way you live? You keep doing the same dumb things, and then you pass those actions down to your kids like they're important! How long is it going to take you to figure all this out?!"

I didn't know what to say. She really was a very smart dog.

The cab slowed and then stopped in front of our building. I set Twix on the sidewalk as I paid the cabbie and then closed the cab door.

"This place is inhospitable," Twix declared, surveying the side-walk in front of our door.

"You mean our block? Or New York City?" I asked, digging my key out of my purse.

"I mean the world," she said.

"I guess that's why we make homes," I said.

I was having trouble finding my key with the dog carrier, my purse, and the leash in my hands. I felt Twix jump up and drag her front paws along my calf.

"Thank you for taking me into your home, Shelly," she said, sounding emotional.

I was surprised. "Twix, this is your home, too," I said. I set down my things to see her better. She was trembling. I picked her up and she curled into my chest. I kissed the smooth fur on the top of her head and thought of her, tiny, sleeping in the ripped newspaper in the puppy store window.

"When you have to wait for people to decide to take you in, you never forget it," she said sorrowfully as I opened the door.

A WEEK LATER, CLEMENTINE and I went to Florida to visit my mother at Hamptons Woods. I sat next to her bed, thinking of all the ways she had helped me. I survived my babyhood. She wiped my ass. She fed me and bought me clothes and took me to school and found agates with me and did a thousand other difficult tasks. I thanked her for it all in some ways, but really, is there any truly adequate way to thank a person for keeping you alive? You thank them by going forward in your own life and trying not to be an asshole. I think Mother Teresa said that, too.

Clementine was fond of Hamptons Woods. She was able to make hot chocolate from the packets they provided in the lobby coffee machine. As Clementine ran back and forth down the halls, spilling hot chocolate on her summer sundress, I tried to get my mom to reminisce about her life. With every visit, she got quieter. The only subject that retained her interest was the farm of her Michigan childhood. She had tried so hard to get away from her farm girl past, but now that she was nearing the end of her life, it was her favorite topic.

"I think everyone should spend time on a farm," she said with a sigh, gesturing expansively at the climate-controlled air in room 204A. She had been telling me about the time she had seen a baby goat be born.

I had never met a baby goat, only the cashmere sweaters provided by their parents. Clementine came back in and sat down, sipping from her Styrofoam cup demurely as she reached for her manual on how to survive an alien attack. My mother looked at her affectionately.

"There's a little box in the top drawer there," my mother said to me, gesturing to her dresser. "Get it for me."

I opened the drawer and found a navy-colored ring box I recalled from my own childhood. I handed it to my mother, and she opened it, then turned the box around to show me. It was the diamond ring she had inherited from my father's mother. She had never worn it because she was afraid someone would steal it from her.

"I want you to keep this for Clementine," she said, handing the box to me. I looked at the stone. It was hard to believe something so sparkly came from deep inside the ground.

Clementine was engrossed in her alien invasion defense plans. I decided I would tell her about her lucky rock later.

I was grateful to my mother for this gift. I turned it over in my hands. "Thanks, Mom," I said. "It reminds me of the agates you used to pull out of the creek for me when I was little."

She looked surprised. "I remember that." She beamed at me. "That was fun."

I took her hand. "Do you remember the time I bought those fake turquoise rocks at Wall Drug?"

She furrowed her brow, then grinned. "Oh, you were really disappointed," she said.

"The agates made up for it, Mom," I replied, and reached for her hand.

3

THE BEACH HOUSE was finally in process as a thing-in-the-world. George and I didn't go out and make any site visits, though. We didn't see the hole they had dug for the pool or the pit where they had put the septic tank.

We heard from Bea by email when there were problems. Bea emailed when Stan had started work too early in the morning, or when Stan's team had failed to close the required safety gate, or when Stan had worked on a Sunday, which was against the rules.

My reply to Bea was always the same: Thanks for letting us know.

Marianne loved that we were not hovering clients. We just let her and Stan work. So aside from Bea's annoying messages, the whole process went really smoothly, mainly because we mostly ignored it.

Soon enough, though, Marianne called to say that the four containers had been loaded onto their four flatbed trucks and were starting their journey. They would be on our tick farm the next morning for their hookup. But not that kind of hookup, ha-ha.

When I went to bed that night, I could not sleep. I imagined our four containers in their caravan. I saw them stopping overnight at a crappy rest stop. They had no hotel room to go to; they were just parked along the side of the road. Our house was unhoused.

That morning, I got up before anyone else and made coffee in our yellow kitchen on West Twenty-Seventh Street. I clutched my device as Marianne started sending me pictures of our containers arriving at the tick farm. George and I had decided we couldn't be there in person to watch them get put into place. It would be too close to watching a cat climb up a vase-filled shelving unit. We would have to be sedated, we agreed, in order to see our house dangling from a crane, getting dropped into place by the force of almighty gravity. Also, I thought Bea might call the cops on the entire procedure, and I didn't want to be there for that, either.

Marianne sent us pictures all morning long, and Stan and his team of workers were all smiling in them, and if our house didn't seem to be smiling, exactly, she looked at least tolerant, like a dog who relents to being dressed up in doll clothes and propped up at a table for a tea party by its child-owners.

We waited to see the house in person until a few days later, after it was all over. We loaded the kids and Twix into the rental car, packed a bunch of snacks, and set off.

I did not understand why I felt sad. This was something I had anticipated for so long, and now the moment was coming when I was about to discover if what was inside my mind was also outside it. But it felt weirdly like a death. It seemed wrong to be excited about it. George turned on the radio, and I tried to bury my feelings under the sound of country music.

We were just passing the Shinnecock monument, this time telling us to not drink and drive, when we heard it: "Side effects of Placatrex are uncommon and include hemorrhoids, hypnagogic hallucinations, and vascular ischemia caused by thrombosis."

"Goddammit!" George cried. "They didn't use my voice!"

He was still fuming as we approached the tick farm. It was there, looming: a giant black box on a construction site. It didn't rise up in the air with quite the Vegas-style majesty of the Shinnecock monument, but it was definitely a presence. The long side of the container, all black, with only one small window in it, reminded me of the side of a barn. I made a note on my device to see if I could figure out how to rent out the side of our beach house to advertise whatever was the contemporary equivalent of Mail Pouch Tobacco. Maybe Caring bars.

Marianne was there to meet us, smiling, and Tim was there because I had asked him to do a shaman blessing. Tim was not smiling. Probably because he was busy engaging his core.

Vinnie and Frank weren't there because they had gone back to Vermont right after dropping the containers off. They were moving to the Hamptons. They had found a little rental house close to the dump and were excited to see what kind of contracting work they could get among all these rich people.

I walked inside the shipping container that was now my house. Was it still a container, or was the container only my house's backstory?

Jack and Clementine were running between the micro bedrooms, claiming which teeny room they wanted. George and Marianne were in the kitchen. I left them and headed to the stairs to take a look at our bedroom.

As I ascended the stairs, I felt like a woman in a classic movie. I wasn't just a real housewife, I told myself, I was like someone in an advertisement: a Real Housewife! I was in my beach house, where I was going to let everything go, where I was going to get away from everything unpleasant, where I was going to forget that the process called living was intrinsically connected to dying. Finally!

I walked into the bathroom to see our Japanese toilet. I saw a toilet there, but it was a regular one. No buttons, no remote control.

I came out of the bathroom. George was standing there, admiring the bedroom, chatting with Marianne.

"WHERE IS THE JAPANESE TOILET?" I yelled.

Marianne straightened up in alarm. "What?"

She went into the bathroom and inspected the regular toilet. She lifted the regular lid and peered inside. She poked at the regular handle. She crouched down low on the floor to read the regular lettering stamped on the underside of the regular bowl. I stood right behind her, fuming.

"I was sure we had ordered it . . ." Marianne trailed off.

I felt like I was a berserk raccoon leaving my sooty paw prints on the ceiling. How could they have forgotten my Toto? My *Toto*! Toto the dog had made it from home to Oz and back, but *my* Toto could not make the simple journey from the Japanese toilet factory to my not-a-trailer bathroom? I felt my hands opening and closing around the house keys I was holding. I threw them across the room. They hit the wall and made a black mark.

"I'll call Vinnie and Frank now," Marianne said, retreating hastily.

George came up the stairs. I hoped he hadn't heard the keys hit.

"You're acting like a real princess asshole right now," George observed.

"I'm frustrated!"

"Shelly, this is just lifestyle creep!" George chided. "Get a hold of yourself!"

I whirled around and stormed out of the house, making snorting sounds, like a dog doing a reverse sneeze. I walked into the yard of our house, which was not a yard, because there was no grass there yet. It was still a construction site, with big piles of dirt beside the hole that had been dug for the pool and the hole where the septic tank had been buried. There was bright orange safety fencing around the entire .49 acres, to keep the tick-riddled deer from frolicking there, I guessed.

I sat on a boulder in the dirt. I was like a toddler having a tantrum, I knew, but I couldn't stop it. I, the person who cared for people, had decided I was tired of it, and wanted to be cared for myself. And if I couldn't get anyone else to do it, I would outsource the job to a Japanese robot named after a dog. And now I couldn't even get that done. The whole unfairness of the system I was not working in seemed to be mocking me.

I pulled my knees up under me and sat there, breathing and listening to the birds. I imagined myself flying overhead, seeing this all from the treetops.

After a few minutes I stood up and walked back to the rental car and sat there. I reminded myself what my backstory was: nothing truly terrible had ever happened to me, and I was being permitted by forces I did not control or understand to float along in my life like I was on the lazy river at Atlantis. But it didn't feel like I was on the lazy river at Atlantis. It felt like I was struggling every second to do the simplest things, like build a beach house I liked out of garbage, when other people seemed to do this so easily. And for them, it turned out great.

Eventually I saw that Marianne was talking to Tim and then getting into her car to leave. Tim left also—no shaman blessing today. The kids and George then joined me in our rental car. I ignored everyone as George drove home, and my family left me in silence, except for Clementine, who piped up to tell me that mistakes are how we learn and George told her to be quiet.

It started to rain hard. Our progress on the Long Island Expressway was excruciatingly slow. When we finally got back to our apartment, Stan called me. He would be in the beach house tomorrow, he said, to address a problem that had just come up.

"What is it?" I asked.

"The basement is flooded," he said.

I put my head in my hands. "How much water is there?"

"Ah, about two feet," he said.

I started to cry.

Stan tried to be reassuring. "Let me tell you, with new houses? This stuff happens," he soothed, like a country crooner. "This stuff happens all the time."

4

AT LEAST I knew what to do with myself. It wasn't like I had never been disappointed before. It wasn't like I had never been tricked into thinking I was buying something magical and valuable that then turned out to be a bag of rocks.

I just kept working. I was fortunate in that I had many new jobs to keep me busy. I had to furnish the house, for one thing. But that was a joyless activity now because I wasn't furnishing it for me, I was furnishing it for the renters we would need to get immediately. I was picking out stuff that was inexpensive and could survive strangers' indignities, like I was just another American multinational hospitality company furnishing another one of my cookie-cutter properties.

A few things from our apartment could go to the beach house, I decided, so I packed them up and then called some movers to put the boxes and pieces of furniture into their truck. I arranged to meet them at the beach house the following morning.

I took the train out to the beach that afternoon with Twix and then I took a cab to the house. Twix and I stayed in the house overnight on an inflatable bed I had brought in a backpack.

The sun shone in and woke me up at 5:00 a.m. because there were no curtains. At 5:30 I heard a truck come to take away the port-a-potty that had been sitting in our driveway for months for Stan and his workers. I watched the truck's robot-arm lift the port-a-potty from our driveway onto the truck bed. The driver strapped it onto the truck bed like a baby into a car seat and then drove away. It felt like a milestone: the house was potty-trained.

Stan had kept his coffeemaker on the counter and some of his ground coffee was in the fridge, so I made coffee for myself at the break of dawn. I had not yet furnished the house with cups or mugs, so I drank black coffee out of the pot as I sat with my dog on the steps of my new house at six o'clock in the morning.

The movers came a little later and unceremoniously dumped the boxes in the house, breaking some dishes in the process. I wasn't upset. The renters would break more, I was sure.

I began unpacking the rest of the items and then a few hours later George drove up with the kids in a rental car. He had said he was going to bring some essentials for us that I hadn't packed. That was the word he used: "essentials." I hadn't asked him what the essentials were, but I was curious.

Shower caddies in our bathrooms were what George thought was essential, as it turned out. I was flummoxed by this. How is a shower caddy even a thing in the world? I thought. Who duped humanity into thinking that you needed shelves—those things again!—in the shower, to hold your stuff? I mean, hello, there is a force in the world called gravity, which will very reliably keep your multiple bathing products anchored to the floor. Why can't you just set your shampoo on the floor? Is it really that inconvenient to have to bend over to get it? Do shampoo and body wash have to be at eye level? Is that so that you can worship them? Is a shower caddy really an altar? If so, who or what are we praying to? Is it body wash? Is it shower caddies? Is it the act of elevating objects? Is this our greatest human power, to lift things up? If so, why don't we lift other people up as easily as we lift up shampoo? Why don't we act as if lifting up people is as essential as lifting bathing products? Why don't we lift up all people, so we can look at them in the eye instead of stepping over them and saying we didn't know they were there? Is putting shower products on the floor and bending over to reach them an act that makes us too vulnerable for our comfort and that is why we created shower caddies? Are shower caddies an insurance against "dropping the soap," like you reportedly have to guard against doing in prison? Is the idea that if you have a shower caddy, you will not be vulnerable to rape and violence? Does this somehow tie into the fact that body wash that is marketed to young men is given ridiculous names like Swagger? Is Swagger made so my son can worship it in the shower caddy altar and not worry about bending over and being vulnerable while he does? Is the larger purpose of shower caddies that they enable prayer to Swagger without kneeling or bowing? Isn't it strange that positions of worship like kneeling and bowing are also sexual positions? If this is what shower caddies enable, are they somehow actually working against the fostering of humility that is a bedrock of worship in every religion? Are shower caddies what we come up with when we want to believe in powers greater than ourselves but not in powers that can humiliate or harm us?

With our shower caddies accounted for, George, Jack, and I then spent the next few days making the beds. That is, we made the beds with screwdrivers and Allen wrenches because the beds were cheaper and more sustainable if you bought them unassembled. We got the kind of beds with drawers underneath them, which made the assembling pretty challenging. But we needed drawers for storing stuff because there had only been room for one closet in the entire house.

We sweated and swore and put the beds together. "We" meaning everyone except Clementine, who, to my relief, had left her book about the *Challenger* in the city. She amused herself by playing a game on her device where half-dressed women who needed to poop were able to use the toilet once you helped them by playing Scrabble. Then, when I told her that game was inappropriate, she played another one where women sat on washing machines and drank wine.

By Sunday night, we all had beds; we had showers with shower caddies; we also had a thousand boxes to throw away from the way our sustainable, unassembled beds had been packaged. I called Stan and asked him what I should do with all the bed garbage. We hadn't figured out garbage collection at the beach yet. He said he would get us a five-hundred-gallon container to throw all of it in and then he would have his guys come and take it away.

The container was delivered to our driveway later that week, dropped right where the port-a-potty had been. It would have made the perfect hot tub for our shipping container house, if we hadn't immediately started throwing trash in it.

One thing I learned, sleeping in the house for the first time, was that I hadn't anticipated how much the house would feel like being on an airplane. Everything about the house was small and narrow. I had had to buy tiny garbage cans for every room in the house, but the tiniest ones of all were for the bathrooms. The garbage cans in the bathrooms were each smaller than a basketball-shoe shoe box. They seemed to be overflowing with garbage every few hours, especially because at least one of my family members had the annoying habit of taking a Caring bar into the bathroom and eating it while on the toilet, causing the garbage to quickly fill with wrappers.

The result was that whenever I sat on the toilet in the bathroom, I was sitting next to the tiny, overflowing garbage can. It felt strangely like I was living on a cross-country flight that would never land.

5

WALKING ON THE beach, I picked up a rock about the size of a nectarine, pale pink and shot through with sparkles. I threw it in the water like it was a softball. It was the first time I had thrown something in a while without being in a rage. I watched the rock arc, heard it kerplunk, and saw the backsplash came up, like a small whale had exhaled.

There, I thought. I had moved the world a little.

I was walking Twix, looking at my device. Jack had messaged me that Marianne said she couldn't use him as a summer intern but suggested he reach out to Vinnie and Frank.

What do you think? Jack texted me.

That could be good, I messaged him. I didn't want to tell him that I could hardly believe how hard it was for him to find a job when he wasn't even going to get paid for it.

Walter popped into my mind. I took out my device and texted him a picture of Twix sniffing a dead fish. Walter was one of my few non-pet-owning friends who genuinely liked dogs.

Nice! he wrote.

Are you in the studio? I asked.

Yep.

What are you working on?

He sent me a picture of the new painting: a giant salad, bright with tomatoes and cucumbers.

Wow! I added. What happened to the paintings of cash?

You can only follow your own path, he replied.

I put a heart on that.

Sadly, he added.

6

THE DOORBELL AT the beach house rang. I hadn't heard the beach house doorbell before. It played the opening line of Woody Guthrie's "This Land Is Your Land," which was also the melody of the Carter Family's "When the World's on Fire," because Guthrie pinched it from them.

Maybe it's one of our new neighbors coming to say hello, I thought, because I am insane with hope when it comes to other people.

I opened the door and saw Alice's black sedan in the driveway, but not Alice. A different white woman in a sleek black ensemble stood in the doorway in taupe-colored heels. "Has anyone ever approached you about using your house as a location for movies or TV?" the woman asked.

My first thought was that George, having worked in advertising, might know something about this. But he was at the hardware store getting a skimmer because Clementine was shrieking about bugs in the pool, and even if I texted him, I knew he wouldn't answer right away. He wasn't attached to his device like I was, as a tool for communicating, maybe because it wasn't his job.

"No," I said, looking at her suspiciously.

"Well, I'm a location scout and this house would be a great place for a shoot," she announced. She looked around admiringly as she handed me her card: Samantha Hopkins, Perfect Locations. "This is a container house, right?"

I nodded and let her in.

She walked into the living room, taking in the view. "Are the containers used?" she asked hopefully.

Suddenly, I understood. She wanted to hear the terrible backstory.

"Oh, yes, the entire house is upcycled, I mean, recycled. I mean, *rescued*," I said.

"Incredible," she said, looking into my eyes in a way that reminded me of Cat.

I knew how to hold a gaze now, if money was in the cards. "The shipping containers themselves were rescued from China," I said. "They were filled with shelves."

"Shelves . . ." she mused, as if she was trying to figure out how that added to the appeal. Goddammit, Marianne was right, I thought. I should have gone for the chicken nuggets after all.

"What about your pool?" she asked, eyeing it from the living room window.

"Solar powered," I said casually, by which I meant that there was no heater.

"This is *wild*!" she said, tapping into her device. "Can I send my colleague Sandy over to take some pictures? Then I'll list it and find clients for you."

"Can you give me a ballpark figure of how much we could make doing this? I want to make sure it's worth our time." I was proud of how those words came out.

"Oh, I thought I had gone over that already," she said.

"No," I said. I smiled politely.

"Well, sometimes these locations can command really high prices," she said conspiratorially.

"Yes?" I cocked my eyebrow.

She said a very large number.

I smiled. The big secret to making money, I thought, is that you have to already have it.

7

"JACK, COME WALK to the beach with me," George said.

"Right now?" Jack was working on his college essay. The prompt said he should write about overcoming a hardship. I figured I would let Mr. Rudge handle it.

"Do you want to come with?" Jack asked Betty, who was sitting across the living room, doodling something in her notebook. She was visiting for the weekend.

"I'll stay here for a bit," she said. "You go ahead."

Jack and George left. Clementine was in her room. I was shopping on my device for spill-resistant decorative pillows for the couch as part of an activity that I had begun to think of as renter-proofing.

Betty and I weren't often alone together. I tried to strike up a conversation. "Is that a diary?" I asked her.

"No," she said. "I'm writing a book."

"Really?! What's it about?"

She looked down shyly into the lap of her trash bag romper. "*The Ethical Guide to Becoming a Gazillionaire*. It's about how to accumulate wealth in an ethical fashion."

"What's the secret to *that*?" I asked, looking at Twix and hoping she was listening.

"You have to love making money but you can't be attached to it," Betty explained.

"That's sounds pretty difficult," I observed.

"That's what's going to make my book so great," she said, tossing her hair. It was her natural color today, black. I had to admire her confidence.

Betty stood up, holding her not-a-diary to her chest. "Don't get me wrong, I love visiting your beach house," she declared. "But the idea that you bought this land and built on it and now you think this whole thing is yours?" She chuckled. "Well, I just think that's ridiculous. The Native Americans had it right. People can't own land; it outlives us. Sovereignty is an illusion. The only true control comes from within."

"Did you just make that up?" I asked.

"No, my friend Sarah said it. She's a stand-up comedian."

Jack ran back into the house. George was a few steps behind him, carrying a surfboard. I was relieved for the distraction.

"Where did you get *that*?" I asked George.

"The house where I got the bike."

"Nan and Bob's?"

"The big house at the end of the street. I don't know who lives there."

I had met Nan and Bob on the beach with their daughter, Violet. They lived right beside the water in a gorgeous ranch.

"Why do you keep picking through their trash?" I demanded as George set the board down on the couch.

"They have the best garbage! Look at this, it's top quality!"

He ran his hand over the finish.

"George, they undoubtedly have security cameras! They'll see you digging through their stuff!"

"That's why I take Jack," he said. "So I can blame him. I can say my kid begged for it."

Jack looked at me, rolled his eyes, and grabbed Betty's hand. They went outside.

I was upset that George had been oblivious to social mores regarding trash, and I was more agitated than I would have been otherwise, having just endured Betty's salvo. "George, garbage in the Hamptons doesn't work like that! It isn't the same as garbage in the city! You have to read the garbage room! You can't just dig through people's trash out here!" I looked at the ceiling, defeated. Nan and Bob were going to gossip about us to all their raccoon friends, I just knew it.

"No, you've got it all wrong," George protested. "I'm setting up a store."

I looked at him, confused.

He held out his device to show me.

I looked. There was the merch—the sweaters and the Noguchi not-an-ashtray among them—beautifully photographed, with descriptions and prices. I was shocked. George was someone who fell into things already built. Not someone who built things from scratch.

"This is just the first step," he said. "I want to open a brick-and-mortar store after this takes off." His eyes twinkled. "I put it on my vision board."

I hugged him. I was proud. But at the same time, I could hear a little voice-over voice inside me saying, There is no way you are going to be able to survive in this area on sweater and ashtray money.

8

SAM CALLED BRIGHT and early in the morning to say her photographer, Sandy, could come tomorrow if I was ready.

"I'm ready," I said.

I wasn't ready. I began cleaning the house. I wanted my house to look amazing for the shoot. The house was serving as a proxy for me. The house would be photographed while I was not. The house would be visible while I remained hidden. The house would make the perfect stand-in for the woman of the house, who didn't really live in it.

I hauled the garbage to the giant can we kept outside. I had learned this lesson about the Hamptons just this week: there is no trash day in East Hampton. You don't put your trash out in a bag on the sidewalk because there is no trash pickup. This was a foreign concept to me as a resident of New York City, because in the city, garbage is simple: people make it all day, and the sanitation department picks it up all night. In the Hamptons, garbage does not work like this. You take your garbage by yourself to the recycling and disposal center, aka, the dump.

I had never learned about this when we were renters at Chez Craigslist, as we benefited there from the service the homeowners had paid for already. One of my first tasks as a new homeowner in East Hampton, then, was to drive my bags of Caring bar wrappers to the dump.

The dump was in the heart of The Springs rather than in the tonier parts of town, so it was only a few minutes away from us. With my black bags in the back of the rental car, I drove through the gate, showed the attendant the Springs dump sticker I had purchased, paid my dump fee, and then parked beneath the sign that read TOWN RECYCLING CENTER beside a picture of a smiling raccoon wearing overalls, as if my chimney raccoon had finally quit drinking out of the toilet and gotten a job.

I stood there with other Hamptonites in what was essentially my first communal-based task, if you don't count getting yelled at for my taste in architecture by my neighbors in the home-owner's association. I opened my garbage bags and went through the painstaking process of putting every bit of my garbage into the appropriate place with its garbage friends. The paper went into the paper dumpster and the metal and glass in the metal and glass dumpster and the plastic in the plastic dumpster, etc. I did all this while vulture-size seagulls screamed overhead and the stench threatened to overpower me. It was like a preschool interview in hell.

I couldn't imagine the billionaires of the Hamptons going through this procedure, so I researched, and I soon found out they didn't, of course they didn't. They dealt with their garbage, like so much else, by throwing money at it. Because if you pay Larry's Carting enough money, they will come and take all your garbage away and *sort it themselves*. I contemplated it: throwing all your crap into one garbage can like you had time traveled back to garbage—

Tudor era England! Next thing you know I'd be throwing my gnawed-on chicken bones in the street!

Now I pay Larry's Carting and I do not fact-check what they do with my garbage. I only know they operate like it's showbiz: they take it away.

9

THE BEACH HOUSE was still wetting her basement pants whenever it rained. I called Stan to come over and look at the problem again.

"Whew, it's hot in here," he said, coming into the living room from the basement to talk to me. "Don't you use the AC?"

We had AC, but running it was expensive. "I prefer the fan," I said.

I took him over to see a crack that had emerged in the living room wall.

"We can repair that," he said. "But you should know that that is going to happen, especially if you don't use AC."

"What's the AC got to do with it?" I asked.

"It's a metal house," Stan said. "Heat makes it expand."

I hadn't thought about that. It was weird to think about the house expanding and contracting, like it was breathing, like me.

Stan nodded, patting the wall gently. "The house wants to move," he added.

"Well, the house needs to sit and stay," I said briskly. "Because I don't want there to be any issues for the renters."

"Oh, you're renting your place out?" Stan asked. He had begun filling out an invoice for me.

"We're trying," I said. I had both Alice and Sam looking for renters for me. I was anxious about getting someone quickly.

"It's quite an unusual house for this area," he said diplomatically.

"So I've heard," I said.

"People around here are partial to barns," he added.

"Yeah, 'modern' barns," I said. "Which means barns that appear to be falling down but inside are loaded with every conceivable technological gadget."

Stan smiled broadly. "People like pretend poor out here," he acknowledged, patting the wall again tenderly as he handed me the invoice. "Not real poor."

10

I WAS UP EARLY the next morning, thinking maybe I needed a new vision board. I wouldn't be trying to manifest anything complicated like a beach house, though—no Pantone chips, no bathroom tile. Now, I just wanted money. Cash, gold, Bitcoin, ducats, whatever. I didn't care what form. Money.

Twix sat in front of me. She held the leash in her mouth expectantly. She loved going for walks on the beach.

"Busy," I said to her. I had returned to reading *Think Your Way Rich*.

"What does that word even mean?" she asked, dropping the leash. "'Busy'?"

"It just means I don't have a lot of extra time to walk you now," I said, putting the leash on her and taking her anyway because I wanted to talk to her. She hadn't spoken to me in a while.

"Who has 'extra' time?" she asked, as I grabbed some poop bags and a dog cookie. "Doesn't everyone just die at a point that's not negotiable unless they kill themselves first?"

"Um, yes," I said.

"Then what are you talking about?"

"I just mean I don't have a lot of free time right now. I don't have a lot of downtime."

"What is 'downtime'? Why are your words so weird?"

We stepped outside. I inhaled. I couldn't believe how good the air smelled out here at the beach. It smelled fresh, sweet. This was probably what money smelled like, when it was right off the press, before it got all the cocaine and pneumonia all over it.

"Free time! Downtime!" Twix continued, sniffing. "It's all made up!"

"It's just how people talk," I said. "You don't understand."

"No, *you* don't understand," she said, dipping to pee by the side of the road. "You live every day until you don't live anymore! That's why time is precious!"

I looked up at the sky. The clouds were fluffy, like Twix. I could see so many Twixes prancing in the air, refusing to come when I called.

Twix stopped to sniff at some leaves. We were in the middle of our quiet Crashing Sound lane.

"Twix, do you think it's possible to be an ethical gazillionaire?" I asked her.

"What's a gazillionaire?" she asked, walking again.

"A rich person," I said.

"No. And that's why *you're* not ethical."

I was annoyed. "Listen, Twix: I vote, I volunteer, I donate, I'm not a Scrooge! What else do you want me to do?!"

"Give all your money away," she challenged, stopping in her tracks. "Not, like, some small percentage. *All.*"

"Besides that," I said quickly.

She scrutinized me. Her gaze could be disconcerting. "You could start by not joking about the fact that I was on sale," she said.

Her words hit me. I bent down to pick her up. "I'm sorry," I said, nuzzling her fur. "I won't do it again."

She licked my face. "Talk is cheap," she said. "I'm watching you."

11

S AM THE LOCATION scout had been bringing potential renters to the beach house, but no one had made any bids yet. Alice had also brought some prospective renters through the house, most recently a family from the city with triplet toddlers—but they didn't like it.

After they had toured the house and left, she told me later, on-screen, what Stan had already told me in person, which was that people come to the Hamptons to rent their fantasy Hamptons house, and that fantasy house, strangely, is not an eco-friendly tin can with a lukewarm backstory. No, it's a fake, falling-down barn with business-grade internet.

I decided that this was the moment to tell Alice that I was also working with Sam to see if I could get renters for film or TV—that I was looking for either residential or commercial renters. I was looking for anyone with money, basically. I had been worried about telling Alice this fact because I had learned that brokers could be territorial. But she didn't take offense.

"Those film and TV people can be really hard on your house," she said, fingering her necklace. She had moved on from the pendants, it seemed. This one was a minichandelier made of stones that were painted to look like blue and green eyes.

"Harder than triplet toddlers?" I asked.

"Just let me know what happens," she said.

Later, Sam called to tell me that a furniture company widely known for its ethics lapses had contacted her and asked to scout the house for a print ad. I had heard of this company. They used child laborers to make the cages migrant children were being put in when they were detained.

"*Really?*" I grumbled to Sam. "*These* are your clients?"

"You can tell them no," she said. "But if you're going to do that, you better do it now. Because they're only in town for the afternoon and they want to come by in two hours. Do you want them to come or not?"

We had no other prospective renters. I didn't want to sell the house. "Bring them over," I said.

I tidied as best I could. The smallness of the house really demanded that you be on top of your clutter. I was starting to appreciate how airplanes had so many built-in storage spaces. When you have a really small house, a cup sitting out on a coffee table looks like a mess.

We went out to get groceries so the people from the horrifying furniture company could look at the house without our presence. Jack, Clementine, and George stayed in the car with the dog as I walked down the aisle scanning a hundred types of virtuous-sounding bars. I told myself that maybe the furniture company being so awful could somehow be a good thing for us, like maybe they would be willing to pay more *because* they were so awful, the way Exxon paid out all that money after the *Valdez*.

"Bad news," Sam said, after we got home. I was unloading four kinds of ice cream into the freezer because everyone wanted a different flavor. "The scout just couldn't see it."

"See what?"

"The vision."

"The vision of *what*?"

"Your house!"

"Isn't that a location scout's job? To have vision?"

There was a pause. I realized I had to stop sounding so desperate. "OK," I said, taking a breath. "So now what?"

"Well, I do have another client interested," Sam said. "But they don't pay much."

I sighed. "What's it for?"

"A movie shoot. That means they bring a lot more equipment and there's more risk for damage."

"What kind of movie?"

"An indie. That's all I know. Can they come and scout tomorrow?"

"Send them over," I said.

12

SURE, THE BEACH house was "ours" now. But George hadn't had a call for an audition in months, we had taken a loan to get the house up from Tim's banker friend, and we were in debt. We were currently living off savings, which wouldn't last much longer. Plus, our health insurance from the Screen Actors Guild was going to run out because George would no longer qualify for it unless he got a major job in the next two months that would put his earnings at the threshold. If a value-packed meteor didn't fall on us from the sky, in other words, we would have to sell the house to pay for COBRA.

When I thought about it all together like that, it was pretty bad. So I tried not to do that. I told myself this was not a strange way to live. For rich people, I thought, money isn't real. I was rich, I assured myself. I was the definition of rich! Didn't I have a beach house?

We went back to the city for the weekend so I could get a few more decorations from our apartment to brighten up the beach house for prospective renters. George had found some Italian glass at the flea market, from his two favorite dealers, Sara and Jim. Three small red vases by Barbini. I packed them up.

While we were in the city I figured I deserved a treat so I booked a night for me and George at the Boxy. We were short on rewards to get a free one, so I had to pay cash for it. It was sad—I hadn't had to pay for a hotel room in anything but rewards points for years.

It was still a rewarding room, though. Afterward, as we lay there, I wondered if the sex felt any different because we were in a room we had paid for and I had to admit, yes, it did. Everything just felt better in a room that was free.

I mean, there is no real free, I know. But I like to imagine a world like the one Betty mentioned—a world where every bit of land isn't cordoned off, owned, and for sale. I like to pretend that I don't have to pay just to live in the world.

George and I relaxed on the bed before getting in the shower, and I was thinking that I have heard that at the moment of orgasm, you are supposed to be able to feel as if you are one with the world, that the things that divide you and keep you separate dissolve. I have had thousands of orgasms in my life by now, and I have never felt that. An oceanic rush of energy, sure. The dissolution of the world? No.

But I want to feel that. I want to see the real world we are all in, and I want see it all collapse. I want to see it revealed as flimsy, as made of tissue paper and glue. I want to see it pop like a bubble because then I will do something wonderful, which is stop believing in it.

13

S AM CALLED AND said the indie film people loved our place and wanted to shoot the movie there. She told me the dates—it was seven full days of shooting—and said she was still negotiating for the best price.

I was sitting on the couch with Twix, elated. "Great!"

"You have to remember that no matter what the pay is, the fact that the house is going to be used as a location is a great fact to include for resale!" she told me.

"You mean, my house is going to be more desirable now that it's a movie star?"

She laughed.

"What's the film about?" I asked again.

"I've been meaning to talk to you about that," she began. "I want you to know that I am using this information to leverage a higher price for you."

"What information?"

"It's a porn film, Shelly," she said flatly.

I was in shock. "Sam!"

"We didn't know this when they came to scout, but now that we know, you definitely need to get more money. Because they anticipate that the film will be rated quadruple X."

"What's quadruple X?" I cried, as Twix rolled over for a belly rub.

"It's a new category of porn," Sam said. "The director calls it porn *evolved*."

"Porn doesn't evolve, Sam! It's not like Pokémon!"

She exhaled sharply. "It's evolved because it's an ethical, woman-owned porn company!"

Darby flashed in my mind. "Ethical, woman-owned porn" sounded like the kind of business she would start.

"There's something else you need to be aware of," Sam went on. "If you rent your house out as a vacation home, you are supposed to do it through the East Hampton Town Hall, so they can put you on the rental registry. Otherwise it's an illegal rental. The town keeps track of how long people rent their homes out. You're only allowed to do it for so many days a year."

"What does that mean for my movie shoot?"

Twix jumped on the floor and went to go someplace quieter. She didn't like when I was on the phone.

"Nothing. Because we are going to rent the house out for the shoot on the down low. Otherwise you need a permit. And we don't have time to get one, and we don't want the town involved. Are your neighbors uptight?"

"Um . . ."

"Well, we'll just make sure you plant a few extra trees in front of your front windows for privacy. I'll call my tree guy now."

She let me go. I immediately called Alice. She wasn't bothered that Sam had made the deal, rather than her. I was starting to get the feeling that Alice was very well off.

"One more detail," I said to Alice. "It's a porn film."

"Cool!" she replied. "So I assume Sam already told you you're doing the shoot on the down low, right? You're not doing it through the rental registry?"

"How'd you know?"

She chortled. "OK, so here's what you need to do now. Have a big housewarming party."

"Are you out of your mind?" I croaked.

"Don't worry, it will be so fun! You can use my new party-planning service! I'm on my way to an open house now, I'll tell you about it later!"

14

AS AN ADULT in New York City, I have attended an array of purpose-driven parties, the purpose usually being money. As the parent of two children, I have also hosted multiple children's birthday parties that were not about money but still, those parties adhered to the rules of the birthday-party economy.

There was the invite-the-entire-class rule, for instance, or, if that could not be adhered to, then there was the invite-all-children-of-the-same-gender rule. An invitation for a few children, but not all, during the prime birthday-party years was verboten. However tedious they became for parents, these parties were carefully planned, held, and attended. They demonstrated a world where everyone comes together, sings, and shares cake.

I had also experienced the party known as the school auction, which was basically a spectacle wherein these same birthday-party parents dressed up in fancy clothes to mingle in a cavernous hall and be persuaded to slit their money-filled veins and hemorrhage thousands of dollars in front of their drunken, cheering peers.

I was amazed that Alice had become a party planner on top of all her other jobs. Say what you will about Alice: she had drive.

"What the hell, Alice," I said, when we were on the phone again. "All the neighbors hate us. Why would we have a party?"

"All the neighbors don't hate you," she said. "But even if they did, that's exactly why you should have a party."

"But how is a party going to help *that*?!"

"A party is a performance," she explained. "You are performing a ritual in which you are creating goodwill. And you need goodwill from your neighbors so that you don't get ratted out to the town when your house is the set of a porn movie."

"But I don't *want* to invite people over," I wailed, like a toddler birthday girl. "I just want to be left alone without my neighbors getting involved in my business!"

"Those types of thoughts aren't helpful," she reminded me.

We were in my C.B.T. session. I took a breath.

"You have to put yourself in your neighbors' shoes," she said in a calming tone. "From where they sit, you are someone who came in and built a new and different house that not only caused a lot of disruption in their neighborhood, with construction, digging, and a freaking *crane*, but your house is also a new thing, and people don't like new things. Or, well—people *do* like new things. But they like new iterations of *old* things. New *new* things are suspect."

I sighed.

"Listen, I'll help you have the party. It will be great! You should be prepared to spend some money, though."

"Oh, for Chrissakes," I grumbled.

"I mean it," she said sternly. "You're going to have to write some checks. It's the cost of doing business out here."

"What kind of neighborhood-party-slash-bribe *is* this?!"

"It's not a party-slash-bribe! It's a *manifestation*. You are making goodwill appear where before there was dislike and distrust. You can invite Bea! Stan! Marianne!"

I pouted at hearing Marianne's name. "I'm still pissed about my toilet," I said.

"Good lord!" exclaimed Alice. "Are you still holding on to that resentment?!"

"Yes?"

"Stop uptalking, Shelly!" Alice reprimanded. "Are you even sure it was Marianne's fault? If you want it fixed, get it fixed already! Otherwise, move on!"

I hated how Alice was right about everything. "OK," I said.

"Great," she said. "You can also pick up a few things for me if you happen to wander into a Party City."

15

"GEORGE," I BEGAN the next morning, as we sat in the apartment, eating breakfast. "We finally got some people to use the beach house for their film shoot. It's going to pay really well!"

He looked up from his auction sniping program. "Awesome!"

"It's just that it's a porn film."

He blinked at me. "Are you serious?"

"It's really lucrative! We just have to do the first couple gigs on the down low."

"What do you mean, 'down low'?"

I tried to wiggle around the issue. "We just have to stay quiet about it, George. It's not a big deal, it's just because of the way things work out in East Hampton!"

"I don't want to do anything illegal for this house," he said, frowning.

"You're aware that the house is built on stolen land," I said.

"You know what I mean," he said.

"C'mon, it's just this one little shoot!" I pleaded. "If anyone in the neighborhood asks what the workers are doing there, you just have to say they're our cousins."

George looked at me grimly. "I'm going to pretend I don't know about this," he said, returning to sniping.

"OK," I said. "But you still have to come and help me host our housewarming party."

"Remind me why we are having a housewarming party?" he asked, looking up.

"To create goodwill," I said, avoiding his gaze as I sipped more coffee.

"You're nuts," he said, sighing. "But OK."

Relieved, I returned to my laptop. It was my job to send out digital invitations for the party. I couldn't find a housewarming-specific invitation on the invitation site, so I took a Halloween invitation with orange flames on it and replaced the word "Halloween" with "Housewarming."

I had to pay for that edit with fake coins specific to the site. I tapped in my real credit card number to pay for the fake coins. Alice had told me to invite "everyone" to the party. So I went back to one of Bea's old Crashing Sound emails, on which she had forgotten to use bcc. I copied and pasted those emails—about seventy people total—and sent out the invitation to all those people, as well as to a bunch of our friends.

I then took Clementine with me to Party City, which had conveniently opened a location on Thirty-Fourth Street. Alice hadn't told me what, specifically, to pick up for her, so I messaged her when I was there.

I'm at Party City. What do you want?

Anything housewarming, she replied.

With Clementine's help, I soon discovered that there was no housewarming section at Party City. There were lots of things emblazoned with "Welcome Home," but the imagery made it clear that it was a welcome home for a newborn baby or a member of the military.

One thing I will say about Party City: it is highly organized, like the dump. It's divided by theme, so once you choose your theme, you can find all the objects in that theme conveniently grouped together. Everything for your outer space party, for example, is all on neighboring shelves: napkins, plates, cutlery, table covers, cups, balloons, etc.

There is also an entire aisle of candy at Party City. There is no category, no theme, no particular message, for candy. Candy is just there, the alpha and omega of Party.

I let Clementine choose some candy. She selected something called Fun Dip, which is colored sugar that you eat by wetting a sugar stick with your saliva and then dipping the wet sugar stick into the pouch of colored sugar. It's not really candy so much as a sugar delivery system made of sugar. We went to the cashier and paid for it. Clementine began delivering sugar to herself before I had even gotten the change.

In my next C.B.T. session, I told Alice that Party City had no housewarming swag.

"Well, that's disappointing," she said. "Because we need ways to underscore the theme. Parties are really all about storytelling, you know."

"You don't say," I said.

"All the party-planning greats know this," she said. She was using the same tone my mother-in-law used when she explained something to me that I didn't understand but which she considered fundamental, like how to work the remote.

The best news about the party so far was that Alice had hired Vinnie and Frank to work as her caterers. They had moved nearby us in The Springs and were excited for the temporary gig, Alice said. "Hamptons hostesses want 'something different' at their parties," she added, "and Vinnie and Frank can deliver on that."

"What do you mean?"

"I asked them to cater for us in their fursonas."

"Wow!" I exclaimed. "That's awesome, because my son, Jack, is going to intern with them, and his first job will probably be at our party."

"Oh, is Jack a furry, too?" she asked.

"I guess we'll find out," I said.

16

I BECAME A PERSON who was having a party for which I had hired a party planner. If that wasn't a rich-person thing to do, I didn't know what was.

And yet, I felt poorer than ever. It defied reason, like how irrational exuberance creates speculative bubbles that hold up the economy. Betty had mentioned the concept to me one afternoon as she was studying for her economics test.

Our party was on a sunny Saturday afternoon. Vinnie and Frank came over shortly after breakfast to set up the food and the bar. They weren't in their fursonas when they arrived. They were just two young guys in T-shirts. The night before, Jack had showed me what he was going to wear as Vinnie and Frank's furry intern. He had taken one of Clementine's headbands and added hornlike extensions made out of pipe cleaners, which he had embellished with streamers and Clementine's glitter paint.

"What are you?" I asked.

"A buck," he said brightly.

"The antlers look like antennas," I said.

"They're antler-antennas," he said, his eyes twinkling. "I'm picking up signals from deep space."

"Excellent," I said. "What's deep space telling you?"

"Radiate love," he said.

I smiled. Jack must have overheard my mantra.

Alice's tent company workers came to put up the tent. There was real grass on the yard now that Stan had unrolled it, carpet-like, over the dirt. I had dutifully hired the anti-tick people to come and spray it with organic anti-tick spray that smelled like lemon furniture polish. Our Hamptons yard, when it was finally done, smelled a lot like the lobby of Hamptons Woods.

George had decided that our party was the perfect time for him to do a pop-up. He was setting up his merch to the side of Vinnie and Frank. He had a variety of curated collectibles, as he was calling them, spread out on several tables. It was like he had brought a little bit of the West Twenty-Seventh Street rummage sale with us to The Springs. No incense guy, though.

I walked over to Clementine, who had decided that the party was the time to debut her new form of currency: Twix Bucks. She was making the bills by cutting out rectangles of paper and drawing pictures of Twix on them and then adding hearts and stars. The plan was to give them to all the guests as they arrived.

"Will people be able to use Twix bucks to buy anything?" I asked her. "They could be like drink tickets at the school fair."

"No, this isn't money like that," she said. "It's just for everyone to be rich with."

"Got it," I said, as I saw Alice walking across the lawn. She had come over early to make sure things were going according to plan. To my shock, Cat was with her.

"Hey!" I said when I saw Cat. "You left Buenos Aires!"

Cat smiled as Alice looked at me quizzically.

"Didn't I tell you we got back together?" Alice asked.

"It didn't come up in session," I said, keeping my face straight.

"Cat is partnering with me in my party-planning business," Alice announced.

"You should offer your readings at parties," I said to Cat.

"I can offer some today," she said. "I have my cards with me. Consider it a housewarming gift."

"I'd love that!" I exclaimed. "I'll set up a table for you by George."

Alice and Cat headed to check on the food. I walked past Betty, who was sitting by the pool. She had come for the weekend, bringing a remarkable array of garbage-bag clothing with her. She had spent the morning wandering around the house, burning sage—it was definitely sage and not Dragon's Blood, I checked—while wearing a bikini that looked like two purple-tinted sandwich bags. Clementine had trailed behind her quizzically, always interested in anything that could ward off catastrophe. She and Betty were friends now. They were busy making Twix Bucks together like two enterprising counterfeiters.

Walter was one of the first people to arrive when the party officially started a couple of hours later. He had walked in the door bearing a gift: a mini, eight-by-ten painting of *Stripper Cash*.

"Here's your *Beach House Cash*, Shelly," he said, smiling.

I hugged him. "Thank you!"

Carrying my painting, I led Walter over to meet Cat—I thought it would be good for two painters to chat. Then I walked back in the house so I could set my painting down in a safe place. I stashed it in Clementine's micro bedroom, in her micro closet.

When I came out, Alice was in the kitchen poking at the gift bags she had packed carefully in cardboard boxes. Each gift bag contained a small box of chocolates and a silver metal water bottle printed with the words "The Means" and three symbols—a house, a plus sign, and a fire symbol reminiscent of the flames George had painted on our mailbox. Everyone would understand that "house" "plus" "flame" equaled "housewarming," Alice said. I didn't think so, but I also thought it possible that I was water-bottle illiterate.

"Do not under any circumstances fight with anyone," Alice reminded me under her breath as I walked past her to greet some more guests.

"Yep," I said. But I was nervous.

It was starting to get crowded. I found George at his table chatting with Bob and Nan, our neighbors whose trash he had raided. The three of them were sitting on three green lawn chairs that George had actually taken out of their garbage, refinished, and repainted white.

"I love these chairs," Nan said, admiring them.

I smiled at George. If Nan figured out that she was sitting on her own discarded furniture, she didn't mention it. She was classy like that.

When I got to the door Sam was walking in with a pan of brownies. Clementine hovered over the pan as Sam told me the latest: the film people loved the house and wanted to shoot here regularly. They were willing to pay more for an exclusive arrangement. We would have steady income from their work as long as we could pull it off without being discovered and shut down by the town.

I was ecstatic to hear this news, but it also made me feel more pressure to ensure that this party would go well. I was underprepared to meet my guests. I had invited everyone by simply copying and pasting the emails from Bea's list. I didn't know who half these people were. Except now, because here was Bea, walking in the door.

"I figured you wouldn't mind if I crashed your party," she said.

I saw something flash. Twix was at my feet, looking at me intensely. Then she floated up and rotated slowly over my head like a disco ball.

By the time I stopped looking at her, I found myself handing Bea a drink. I must have gotten it for her. That was nice of me, I thought.

Bea leaned into my ear. "I heard you're going to have a porn film shot here," she whispered. "I can make sure the town doesn't find out, if you want." She looked at me meaningfully. "I have a very low rate," she added.

I had learned how to work in this world, at last. "That sounds great," I replied. "Thanks so much for the offer."

Marianne walked over to me, wearing a stunning, sparkly pink-and-green gown. She could have been headed to the Met ball. "Congratulations on the house, Shelly. It looks fantastic," she said, surveying the living room. "You've done an amazing job with the decor."

"Marianne, this is your party, too. We wouldn't be here without you—thank you!"

"I'm sorry about your Japanese toilet. If you want, I can price them out for you," she said.

"I'll get it on my next house," I replied, waving my hand dismissively. I was happy that I had found a container of generosity within myself. I couldn't imagine having a next house. We would be lucky to keep this one.

I went with Marianne and Bea to get a drink from Frank and Vinnie, who were now tending bar in their fursuits. Frank was a rabbit, and Vinnie was a fox, as I had imagined. They looked great with Jack helping in his buck headgear. As I stood by the bar, chatting, I looked across the yard and saw that Tim was dancing in a corner of the yard, waving a bundle of sticks in the air. He was doing the house blessing he hadn't done earlier, I realized.

I left the bar and walked over to him. As I got closer, I heard him making a "Shh Shh Shhh!" sound.

"Tim! Am I interrupting you?"

"Yes!" He continued dancing.

He waved his sticks vigorously. I saw now that the sticks were lit at the ends. They were smoking.

"OK, I'll catch you when you're done. Thank you!"

He winked at me and continued his work.

I hoped our shaman/lawyer wouldn't set our lawn on fire. I turned around and walked back to the house. As soon as I got to the kitchen, I heard the front door rattle and Darby walked in.

"Hey, I thought you couldn't come!" I exclaimed.

"I took the jitney," she said, using the word people in the Hamptons use when they mean "bus."

Darby was wearing a tank top. I didn't see any funky accessories on her—just her tattoo of a puppy on her left biceps. Twix jumped up to greet her. Darby bent down to give her some pats.

"I have some great news, Shelly," Darby said, putting down her backpack. "I had to haul all the way out here to tell you in person!"

Darby was so all over the place—I was almost afraid to hear her news. I held my breath.

"I'm starting a dog-walking business and I want to know if you'll join me!"

"What?!" I exclaimed. "What happened to fashion?"

"I got my degree. But I don't think I'm cut out to be a designer. I want to work with dogs."

I couldn't believe that she had made this change to something so practical. "What would I do for you? Walk dogs?"

"No, you'll be my manager. You'll help me manage the schedule, the walkers, and the clients. You could work from home. And I'm offering excellent benefits! You'll have health insurance, paid vacation, and a 401(k) with a company match."

I felt overwhelmed. "Do you think I can really do that? I haven't held a real job in years."

"You'll be great at it," she said encouragingly. "You're very organized, and you're good with people."

Good with people?! I couldn't believe someone was saying that about me. I felt my face flush with pride.

"You know how I know?" she added, as she patted the wall gently, like Stan had all those months ago. "Because you got this bananas beach house built."

17

I ASKED DARBY TO give me a little time to think about it. I thought about running to the bathroom to fly some cream into my face, but instead I did something else, which was turn around and leave my own party.

I put Twix on the leash and took off my four-inch heels and slipped on my flip-flops to walk the five-minute walk down the street, past the clubhouse, through the parking lot, and finally, to the beach where Marianne had helped me and George up after the meeting, and where I had since walked with Twix many times.

I let Twix off the leash as I listened to the water and found a place to sit on the sand. Twix sniffed a bit on the sand, peed, and then came over and sat in the lap of my flowery party dress. I petted her. Did I really want to enter the legitimate working world? What would that be like, getting a real job, working for Darby? Would it possibly feel like being more fully alive?

Even as I asked these questions, though, I knew the answer. I couldn't say no. We needed the money.

I threw a rock in the water and watched the backsplash come up, joyful, like a dolphin. I imagined myself sitting at my desk with all my desk accoutrements spread out in front of me: my computer, pens, and paper clips. I got excited as I imagined the office supplies. I could have paper clips shaped like palm trees and sunglasses. I could buy a pink stapler. I would have fun desk accoutrements while I was doing a real job with real clients talking to them about serious matters: dogs!

"What are you thinking about?" asked Twix.

"My new office," I said.

"Where's that going to be?" She sounded alarmed.

"Home."

"Oh, good," she said, relieved. She put her chin on my foot as my device dinged. It was Clementine wanting to know where the chips were, because Vinnie and Frank had run out of chips for the guacamole. I told her that they were on the top shelf of the pantry and then she told me she couldn't find them, which I could have predicted, because children have an uncanny knack for not seeing what you tell them to look at.

I told Clementine to hold on, I would be right there, and then I put Twix back on the leash and walked her off the beach, through the parking lot, past the clubhouse, and then up the street to our house.

But when I walked in the door, I didn't go straight to the kitchen to solve the chip issue. Instead I went up the stairs to our bedroom and opened my laptop.

I could see what my next step was: I was going to have to sell our two-bedroom apartment on West Twenty-Seventh Street and find a three-bedroom apartment in an even less-fancy neighborhood because I would need to use the two-bedroom-apartment money to buy a three-bedroom apartment that included my new home office and all its exciting supplies.

And as I heard Clementine yelling, "Mom? Mom? Do Tolerance crisps go with guacamole?" I was not floating in a tin can far above the world. I was not feeling pain, and I was not feeling no pain. I was alive in my container, and I was making a list.

MUST-HAVES:

2 bedrooms

3rd bedroom/office

High-speed Wi-Fi

Dog-friendly building

Close to dog park

Japanese toilet!

Acknowledgments

Thank you: Monika Woods, Katherine Nintzel, John Hodgman, Walter Robinson, Sarah Afkami, Melissa Robbins, Molly Mac-Dermot, Sherie Rene Scott, Sarah Manguso, Dave Eggers, Jenny Schaffer, Shane Kowalski, Michael Wheaton, Amy Wheaton, Anastasia Higginbotham, Molly Gendell, Andrea Monagle, Renée Jarvis, Gilmore Tamny, Zoë Ruiz, Joan Witkowski, Nanette Lepore, Bob Savage, Violet Savage, Cassie Mannes Murray, Maziar Behrooz, Chuck Gallanti, Rob Jarvis, Eliza Swann, Grace Kredell, and my family, especially Frank.